MISSIONARY POSITIONS

OTHER BOOKS BY KEN RIVARD:

KISS ME DOWN TO SIZE (poetry, 1983).

FRANKIE'S DESIRES (poetry, 1987).

IF SHE COULD TAKE ALL THESE MEN (short fiction, 1995) – Finalist for the 1996, Writers Guild of Alberta, Howard O'Hagan Award for Short Fiction.

MOM, THE SCHOOL FLOODED (children's literature, 1996, revised/ re-issued, 2007).

SKIN TESTS (short fiction, 2000) – Finalist for the 2001, Writers Guild of Alberta, Howard O'Hagan Award for Short Fiction and Finalist for the 2001, City of Calgary, W.O. Mitchell Book Prize.

BOTTLE TALK (short fiction, 2002) – Finalist for the 2003, Writers Guild of Alberta, Howard O'Hagan Award for Short Fiction.

WHISKEY EYES (short inter-connected fiction, 2004) – Finalist for the 2005, Writers Guild of Alberta, Howard O'Hagan Award for Short Fiction.

THE TROUBLE WITH UNCLE KEVIN (children's literature, 2007), published by the Calgary Communities Against Sexual Assault as part of an educational kit and is only available through www.calgarycasa.com

Missionary Positions

Interconnected Short Fiction

Ken Rivard

Black Moss Press
2008

Library and Archives Canada Cataloguing in Publication

Rivard, Ken, 1947-
Missionary positions / Ken Rivard.

ISBN 978-0-88753-448-5

I. Title.

PS8585.I8763M63 2008 C813'.54 C2008-903084-2

Published by Black Moss Press, 2450 Byng Road, Windsor, Ontario N8W 3E8. Black Moss Press books are distributed by LitDistco, and all orders should be directed there.

Black Moss acknowledges the generous support for its publishing program from The Canada Council for the Arts and The Ontario Arts Council.

MISSIONARY POSITIONS is a collection of interconnected short fiction about a workplace called the Daycare Learning Company and the interactions of the staff who work there.

This book is for Micheline, H.P., Annie and Chris, Melissa and Doug, and for all those who have worked with (for) their own Missionary Boss Woman or Missionary Boss Man.

ACKNOWLEDGEMENTS

Portions of MISSIONARY POSITIONS have appeared in an earlier version as a chapbook entitled WORKING STIFFS (Greensleeve Publishing, Edmonton, 1990) and in THE PRAIRIE JOURNAL.

Thanks to Beth Everest for her editorial suggestions.

"Those who write clearly have readers
while those who write obscurely have commentators."

Albert Camus

"Originality is something that is easily exaggerated,
especially by authors contemplating their own work."

John Kenneth Galbraith

I

MISSIONARY FACES

The Missionary Boss was the Principal of a public school called the Daycare Learning Company, a school for students from Kindergarten to Grade Nine. And the thing she dreaded for years was finally happening. More and more staff avoided her.

"You look and act like someone on a mission," Louise the secretary said the other day.

But the Missionary Boss wasn't offended by that remark. They called her the Missionary Boss and Louise was the one who shortened it to MB. "Think of the letters 'MB' as a warning code," she told a staff member yesterday.

And staff thought she didn't know what they were saying about her behind her back. Privately though, Louise wasn't sure what to feel.

"You're not the kind of boss who fools around," Louise told her this morning.

"Meaning what, Louise? You're a secretary! Remember that! I just want the staff to demonstrate self-control and maturity!" MB snapped.

MB walked with intensity and speed, her body bent forward, as if she were forever walking into a storm. And her gait moved sideways, as if the same storm were pushing her that way. She had that ambitious look: rigid face, lips clamped shut, with her eyes focused only on a line of vision that was three to four feet around her. Anything beyond was ignored. MB was productive and did what needed to get done, like last week when she worked all night to complete eight teacher evaluations. Staff knew better than to interfere with her calling.

Her arms swung back and forth with authority, as if she were on manoeuvres. Stabbing at the air, her finger became an hour hand in a hurry and moved in only a clockwise motion. After, she stopped in the middle of a hallway, placed her hands with fan-like fingers on her hips, tilted her head to the left and gave staff a look that asked, "Now, what are you up to?" Often, she stopped a staff member in the hallway or staffroom and said such things as: "Pick that up will you! or "Get in your classroom!" or "Get this done!" or "That's not right!" or "You're late again!"

And MB loved to talk! At meetings, her words had the urgency of someone intending to save lives. A staff member asked: "What can we do to....?" Before the complete question was asked, no one had a chance to catch his or her breath because MB shook her head, leaned forward, twisted her face back and forth and machine-gunned everyone: "Well, you know it's a matter of perception. Perception is reality. Reality is what you've got to change. You'll realize you want to do it my way and... ."

Occasionally, MB's eyes looked downward and swept the

floor, as if as she were looking for a lost ring or earring. In actual fact, that was when she searched for her compassion. After she found her humanity, MB hesitated before looking up because she was unsure of how to expose this tenderness. When in doubt, MB lifted her head, shook her hair and continued on, as if sympathy were a mosquito needing to be slapped.

* * *

"MB looks like the fat chicken cartoon character on TV – the same chicken who constantly tells others to smarten up. Ever notice how the flab on her face and neck slides from side to side whenever MB moves or talks. I'll bet some days she feels so heavy she runs out of breath just crossing her legs!" Angie, a young female teacher whispered to Louise.

Then, Louise's eyes widened and her head motioned to someone standing a few feet behind Angie in the main office of the school. It was MB! Hopefully she hadn't heard Angie's whispering.

"Busy today, Angie?" MB asked.

"When am I not?"

"Watch any cartoons lately?"

"Only with you in them," Angie muttered to herself as she scooted out of the office blushing.

MB's skin was pale and glistened with sweat, especially in the middle of her forehead, whenever she exerted any physical energy or overheard someone like Angie talking about her. When standing close to MB, the air became a perfect mix of sweat and perfume. Her hair reminded everyone of jet-black leaves from a newspaper photo of a tropical puzzle plant. Recently she cocked her head of thick, black hair to one side in order to compensate for diminished hearing in her left ear. MB's hot chocolate-brown eyes were huge and shone behind her black-framed eyeglasses; she looked up the right or left whenever she answered a question and it was difficult to know when she was telling the truth. Then, MB nudged her glasses closer to her face and took another swig from her usual cold can of Diet Coke. And she wore outfits that were far too short and too tight for her thighs, threatening to rip open the skirt she was wearing at any moment. Angie figured that MB spoke from the belly and part of her calling was to make people stand taller just because she was brought up in a German farm family with her two brothers.

Occasionally, MB spoke of her husband whom she met in a New York City nightclub where he was the manager and who now delivered mail in Calgary.

"He's climbed all the mountains he's needed to climb so delivering mail is just right for him now," she said.

"Hope he doesn't get lost delivering letters!" Angie said, the other day.

Then, there were MB's two sons, the second she considered a pure gift from God.

"Doctors said that second boy of mine wouldn't make it but he did," she said to Angie not long ago in the hallway outside the main office.

"He's a fighter – like his mother," Angie replied.

"Am I a fighter to you Angie?"

"No, I meant he's a survivor."

"Oh, right."

During those rare moments, when MB talked about her

private life, staff members loved it because it made them feel they had a chance to enter her inner circle.

On very stressful days, MB uncharacteristically confided in her secretary by crouching down beside her in the main office of the school and almost whispering: "You know something, Louise? Sometimes I feel like an overweight twelve-year-old genius suddenly becoming an adult who would love to run away from her adolescent body, as if a portion of me has never left Grade Six or Seven. I know puberty lasts from twelve until forever but I feel as if I bypassed those years for instant maturity."

And if one bad day stretched into another, MB thought she'd be happiest winning a lottery and running a tiny general store in upper New York State – an idea she shared only with her husband.

Reality again set in yesterday when she said to her secretary, "You know, Louise, sometimes people around here are like resentful children either because they don't get what they want or I'm not behaving the way they want. Have I got news for them!"

If Angie or any other staff member asked, MB told her or him exactly when her own maturity began, what her vices were, and which of her missionary faces she needed most here at the Daycare Learning Company.

* * *

"Sometimes I think of plunking a staff member on my lap with my strong farm hands firmly placed on his or her back and together reading instructions on how to behave.

But as a boss, I don't get paid enough to do this. I'd like to respect these teachers but I end up treating 'em like puppets!

I mean I read feelings to my advantage, particularly when a staff member was alone in my office with me. I could instantly sense dishonesty, fear, pain, resentment, being controlled, resignation and finally, peace. How I did this was fast and thorough: observe quickly and carefully the details of body language – especially the eyes if they avoided mine, and if the hands were sweaty too, because hands had more sweat glands than any other body part. After my initial observing, I tried anything to have the staff member reach resignation and peace after realizing that only I was in charge. After that was accomplished I told the staff member to relax.

Yet, being a multitask person, I was a three-minute miler myself and moved at whatever speed it took to get the job done. In fact, last week, as I was zooming down the hallway, I half-smiled at my secretary when Louise told me she was overloaded with work.

"Just do what's in front of you! You know – first things first! I don't need to show you what to do next do I? No? Good! Look, I'm in a hurry!"

So what if Louise stomped over to the staffroom in silence, her head throbbing with anger and planning to possibly plant a bomb in my bottom desk drawer.

Seems as if I was born in my bottom desk drawer because I am so dedicated to my job and I would probably die in that drawer too; my eulogy will say that I wished I spent more time on the job.

Whenever it was necessary to model appropriate behaviour for a staff member, I made it a point to climb out of that drawer. As a matter of fact, at a staff meeting this morning, I told myself I'd have sex for them too – if need be. Maybe, I could plop them, one by one, on my lap, slide my hand up their blouses or shirts and then down their pants whenever they required directions. I'd move their arms and legs for them too. And I'd make sure their mouths gasped and their heads turned or nodded at precisely the right moment. With their eyes rolling back into their heads, my fingers could demonstrate how pleasure was best achieved by letting someone else do the work.

But the thing I dreaded was finally happening. Because no one understood my intentions, nobody wanted me here anymore. And that's not all!"

* * *

Yesterday, one of the superintendents from Central Office was here. In MB's office, his furious eyes bulged, as if he were playing the lead role in one of those Jim Carey movies. At first, MB just watched and listened.

My name is Angie. I knew I was young but I needed to know how I was doing so I sneaked a look in my confidential file in MB's office while she was away at a conference. Unfortunately, the Assistant Principal, Eric, caught me in the act: "Angie, what are you doing in MB's filing cabinet!" he demanded.

The file contained some unfavorable comments about a questionable teaching performance but the evaluation was written six months ago. I already knew the negative evaluation beforehand but was too busy lurking around to notice the date under MB's comments. First I told one teacher and that teacher told another teacher and on and on:

"You should read what the boss writes about us!"

Anyhow, the superintendent blasted me for my underhanded behaviour!

"ANGIE, I DEMAND THAT YOU GET SOME COUNSELLING!" he shouted.

"But I. . . ."

"NO EXCUSES! THE COUNSELLING BETTER START TOMORROW!"

As I hunched over and sobbed so hard into the sleeve of my white blouse, I felt like I was drowning in my elbow.

"And you better stop by at a drugstore on your way home, Angie. Buy grow-up pills," MB told me.

"I'm so sorry," I sobbed.

When the big boss left, MB briefly became my gentle but insistent mother. Felt like at any moment she would invite me onto her lap.

"We both know that it won't happen again, right Angie?"

"I didn't mean to sneak a look at my file. I was just worried about having a job here next year."

"I understand but you know what you have to do now, eh Angie?"

"Right. I'll call the Employee Assistance Program downtown and check into counselling."

"You can use my phone right now. Let me find the number for you!"

"Here, right now? Are you sure?"

"Couldn't be more sure, Angie. I'll dial."

MB dialed the number and said: "Hold on, I have someone here to speak to you about getting immediate counselling."

Then, I grasped the phone.

"Want me to leave now, Angie?" MB whispered loudly, pointing to her office door.

* * *

Louise just returned a couple of days ago from a magical vacation and already her vacation pictures were developed. It was good for her to get away from her secretary job. Her upper arms felt wonderful because they were thinner and tanned. No longer was her skin prickly or white. Four weeks around her parents' swimming pool in Vancouver had done it for her. She swam dozens of lengths each day and watched her diet carefully. Some days she went to the beach too.

The curling smoke from her cigarette made shapes of muscle men and muscle women in the staffroom air just as MB passed by her and said: "Louise, you look vibrant and your beautiful arms give you away.'"

What was she up to? Who was MB trying to save today? It sounded like she was rehearsing something for her latest mission. Louise clenched her teeth and smiled at MB, as if she were trying to keep the boss's praise in perspective. What did MB want from Louise anyway?

Later, while looking in the mirror in the staff washroom, Louise noticed that her hair was still pushed back in a perfect summer hairstyle and her make up was minimal except for thick ribbons of eye shadow. A new beige dress highlighted her tanned skin and even her eyeglasses were a good match for her new bronzed look. Then, Louise pretended that her two huge corral earrings were trophies she received for healthy living this past summer. After Louise returned from the washroom, MB plopped her hand on Louise's back and she hoped the boss didn't figure out the reasons why she wanted to stay tanned forever. And now she was rubbing each of Louise's biceps in that friendly way women sometimes did with each other. Louise just gritted her teeth and silently asked MB to remove her hands.

Maybe, Louise will just show everyone her vacation pictures. That might get MB's hands off her. Bending over to get them out of her purse, Louise stayed there until she noticed MB moving away from her chair.

Her photographs were mostly of scenery, old buildings, horse races and groups of ocean bathers. Most staff members demonstrated polite enthusiasm for Louise's pictures but they were not sure what to say about the one of her in a wine-coloured bikini. In that photograph, Louise was posing in a white lawn chair. Apparently, the chair belonged to her husband who took this picture, a man made infinitely more attractive because of his skimpy bathing suit. Behind the lawn chair was an aging, sand-coloured building, whose one window had been filled in with brick and concrete. Louise was partially sucking in her belly. And her left arm was half-extended while her fingers pointed at her throat, as if Louise had just finished laughing at a sexy idea. In fact, her lips were swelled and hungry. Even her hair could not decide if it wanted to be red or brown or whatever and was combed down flat, curling just slightly at the neck.

"Say your prayers, MB," Louise whispered to herself. "My skin is in love with the sun and I have a delicious plan for the man behind the camera!"

* * *

Sometimes Angie wore a hurt as big as a half-built house and leaned against the counter in the staffroom kitchen when her chalk-white panties unexpectedly slipped to the floor. Not able to fall asleep all night, Angie worried about her financial status to the point that she actually lost weight. And she skipped breakfast too so it seemed as if her panties simply became too big overnight! Money was tight and she expected a raise on today's paycheque. No such thing! It was tough being a young woman on the dollars she made. She had expenses you know! Other teachers whispered and snickered behind their hands. "They must be talking about me!" Angie thought aloud. "Yet, I'm not that important!"

Earlier today, in a sudden burst, Angie told the MB that as a kid, she once ripped her panties climbing a fence and she didn't want to go home in case she got a beating from her mother. She remembered her mom saying: "Angie, you're going to have to miss a few days of school because I have no thread to mend your panties."

When she finally returned to school Angie wore her older sister's panties, the same sister who died from leukemia two years earlier.

"That's an incredible story, Angie!" MB said with a look that asked Angie if she were looking for a raise, sympathy or both.

What the hell, Angie couldn't pull MB's strings, like MB pulled hers. And quite suddenly, Angie had to laugh at her sister's death; if the sister were alive and saw Angie's panties on the floor; she would have pointed at Angie's crotch, slapped both her thighs and laughed the leukemia into remission.

Not long ago, when money was even scarcer for Angie, she felt tighter than a bull's butt at branding time. She would have joined the armed forces instead of working here at the Daycare Learning Company. That way Angie got a free warm coat to wear in the winter. If she hadn't found a better job, she'd be at home cherishing her armed forces winter coat and shining each button, one by one, until her mother repaired Angie's panties.

Blushing like the warm glow of a toaster, Angie bent down, pulled her panties back up, smoothed her skirt and left her childhood pain on the staff kitchen floor. If MB saw this happening, she would fix Angie's panties with the whitest of thread right there on the spot.

Sometimes Angie wore a hurt as big as a half-built house.

* * *

His name was Eric and he was MB's Assistant Boss. He once worked as a plumber but grew tired of his one-sided talks with pipes. Now, he liked to think he moved through the Daycare Learning Company with the quick step of a wiry man whose ambitions made him want to reach much higher than his five-foot seven stature and show his true colours. Some days Eric aspired to be a superintendent. Other days, he rechecked his sanity and changed his mind entirely.

Last week, Eric overheard Angie saying that he was a bit of a hero because he wanted to look so good at his job – a real showman! Eric told her he loved being a hero and that he couldn't believe he got paid to do this job. Another time someone told Eric he reminded him of a song-and-dance man rehearsing his way to the top of the company. And Eric knew MB sometimes gave him a look that said he was too impulsive or naïve. Occasionally, she chopped him out of the conversation at staff meetings with a snap of her wrist and said: "No, Eric that's not how it is!" She knew how to grab him by the spine, maybe because his spiffy clothes made him more noticeable and easier to grab.

Eric wished other staff members would dress better to look better. He knew his colours, his spring colours. Eric's hair, when not touched up, was the colour of ashes and his eyes were sky blue. He wore light blue and he told other staff which colour or colours they should be wearing but most of them didn't listen. "If only they knew what the right colours can do for a person at work. I mean look, look at me," Eric said to himself one day.

This morning when Eric arrived at work, Angie laughed at him behind a file folder. Eric's face was as red as a STOP sign from the weekend sun. He was hoping that everyone saw that tanning brought out the best in his colours. "I even started jogging yesterday," he told anyone in the vicinity. "You should do the same!"

"Hey, Eric your face looks like a red bulls-eye for your clothes," someone said. And soon more staff lined up for target practice. Eric ducked, weaved and bobbed. He covered his face. More hands went to mouths, like dominoes, one after the other.

"I do feel healthier, though," Eric said

"How are your insides feeling?" Angie asked.

"Not too good right now, Angie."

"Might help to stay out of the sun for a few days."
"Yea, right."
"Ever think of going back to plumbing?"
"Only after too much sun."
"And then what would your skin do?" asked Angie.

* * *

They called her Irene and she was the grandma on staff. She sat in the staffroom with her open hand covering an ear and the fingers from her other hand buried in her hair of gray curls. Her left shoe tapped on the carpet and she was "Hungarian angry", as she often said. That Eric, the resident colour-conscious, assistant boss guy, borrowed her cassette player two days ago and returned it broken. It was Irene's personal machine purchased with her own money. She usually kept it locked up in her filing cabinet in case the school machines malfunctioned. And she wanted to know how her machine got broken. Now! Otherwise, she planned to rip that powder blue shirt right off that smug Eric. Oh! Oh! She suddenly felt her Hungarian accent taking over her English again because that always happened when she became overly upset. Gawd, she hated when her Hungarian butchered her English! When she got up from her desk, she felt as if her printed dress were filled with complaints about her cassette player as she stomped over to MB's office. But the boss was busy, so Irene paced back and forth and her normally barely noticeable limp became more apparent. When Eric walked by, he promised to get it fixed as soon as possible. Irene reminded him that she was not one to "brown nose" around the boss but the machine was very important to her. And she didn't want anything in return – just her machine working again. Also, Irene was retiring soon and she didn't want to leave any loose ends around the Daycare Learning Company, including the idea that her personal cassette machine, which she used to play her Chopin tapes, was broken here.

"Be patient, Irene. I'll get it done today," Eric said.

"You better!" she replied with a clenched fist ready below her chin.

Now, that shrimp was begging Irene to be tolerant and that he'll have her portable cassette player repaired today after work. He must be afraid of what MB might do when Irene told her what happened. Too bad! Tough! Everything had been proceeding on schedule for her upcoming retirement until a few minutes ago when her machine came back unable to store what little Chopin joy she had left.

"Be fixed soon," Eric repeated.

"Yea, sure, Eric! Sure!"

Irene's fingers were stuck, buried in her hair of Hungarian anger while Chopin's Impromptu No. 2 in F Sharp Major, Op. 36 raced from one ear to the next.

"I need a place for my Chopin, Eric!"

"Can't he wait until the end of the day? I can't just drop everything and go to RADIO SHACK right now."

"Eric, his music is all I have! It's the only thing that makes sense around here and I want to retire in peace."

"You'll have Chopin back as soon as I can get the machine fixed, Irene. Promise!"

In the office, the photocopy machine hummed and copied and hummed and copied.

* * *

Every time Angie opened her mouth, her face threatened to tear itself wide-open in slow motion. Recently, she tried to protect her face with baby powder. That sweet-smelling, white smoothness helped Angie's forehead and cheeks relax for some reason or other. Maybe, it was the baby reminder.

So what if Angie was getting a bit fat! She told people at work that she refused to let go of her baby fat because she planned to stay young forever. Angie grew accustomed to wearing baby powder and the staff, especially at parties, started calling her Baby Powder Angie because of that sweet smell.

Today, she told some people at school that she could be pregnant and that she might marry the father of the baby because they were so deeply in love. When she told MB, the boss said: "Angie, I'd like to ask my priest brother to offer a few extra baby powder prayers for you. Something more than what's available on the baby care shelves at WAL-MART or Shopper's Drug Mart. Know what I mean?"

"I think so," Angie replied.

How sweet! MB was not a bad person, even though she usually had her hand in everyone and everything. At the moment, the world was not black or white for her and Angie, for one, didn't want her gone from the Daycare Learning Company yet.

Angie may be expecting. She might marry the daddy. That was no lie. However, the marriage date was still a question mark. The more Angie talked to other staff members about this, the more she felt she was not trapped in her own truth, her own "maybes". Yes, as the day wore on, Angie became more and more philosophical about birth and death. Last week she heard David Suzuki say that society was no longer afraid to talk about all the secrets, except for one – death. Death would not interfere with the maybe birth of her baby. It had better not! And the more Angie felt the ease in her body, the more she smelled the baby powder. Wait, something was moving down there! It was her spine. Had to be those prayers from MB's brother.

"Where's my powder?" Angie said. "Where's my powder? I wanna feel even more pregnant!"

* * *

Nobody at work really knew where Louise got all her money and she wanted to keep it that way. She certainly didn't make a living with her secretary's salary at the Daycare Learning Company. In fact, she told people she sometimes forgot to cash her paycheque from one month to the next. Apparently, she had lots of old money from far-removed relatives in Hong Kong and her husband had a good job. Louise tried having children of her own but her husband's sperm count wasn't up to it so they were considering adoption.

This morning Louise told MB how much she enjoyed eating smoked salmon or caviar or truffles. Even the boss thought that a truffle was a chocolate and Louise had to tell her it was an edible, fleshy, potato-shaped fungus that grew underground, a true delicacy! Some of these Daycare Learning Company people simply didn't know any better!

Louise also loved the taste of the very best French cognac, especially after she had given her annual Christmas presents to a church designated, family-in-need. It was her duty to give and her duty to reward herself with cognac.

Later, at break time, Louise was nibbling on her toast and pâté when Eric casually asked, "Louise, would you like to have children of your own?"

He already knew about her family situation! How dare he do that to her! That smug bastard with his wife and two kids! And she let him have it!

"Who the hell are you to be asking such a question, Eric? How insensitive of you!"

Her pâté threatened to turn back into a liver. In the meantime, Eric was so stunned, he reminded Louise of a salmon swimming in the opposite direction of her. Then, she paused in her rage, her breath like tentative steam and her eyes flitting from floor to walls to ceiling. And Eric became that kid who was never sure if his parents had enough money for Christmas gifts, a kid Louise met only once a year. She hoped.

Nobody at work knew where Louise got all her money.

* * *

Being an Assistant Principal sometimes felt like a shock to Eric. He was first and foremost a computer guy and he probably loved working alone all day in a small office at the far end of a hallway. However, with his new position, he had to interact regularly with staff and Dale Carnegie, he was not. It was Central Office who promoted him and now MB treated him like a naïve, nine-year-old boy. Meanwhile, it seemed like Louise had been coming on to him more and more and he could end up in bed with her. Eric could tell by the way MB acted that she thought he didn't know the first thing about sex, even though he had a wife and two kids of his own. How could he tell? Well, first of all, MB had this annoying way of resting one hand on his back and patting his shoulder with the other. Secondly, she laughed and shook her big head whenever Louise dropped everything to do something for Eric, like finding a file or making a phone call.

Right now, Eric was in his new Assistant Principal's office with the door closed and checking his hair in the mirror behind the door. Depending on the lighting, light blue would be the best way to describe the colour of his eyes. His face was oval-shaped and a bit oily. A new pinch of beard clung to his chin, like a clump of burnt bush. Although his hairline was receding, he didn't try to hide it with long strands of hair combed forward. What hair he had left was combed straight back – two black brackets around a pair of eyes. And his shoulders seemed ready to fold one over the other on his chest. Eric straightened up. It was time to get ready for the staff meeting. Time he cleared his throat and pretended to be an extrovert. His eyes darted back and forth and they became tiny pumps trying to push the more outgoing person inside him to the forefront. He took one last look in the mirror, opened his door and headed to the staffroom.

There, he cleared his throat, called for everybody's attention and asked for more teacher input as to how things were done around here. MB nearly choked on her Diet Coke and gave him a look that would melt the chrome off a trailer hitch. Then she walked up to him and whispered through her teeth into his left ear, "What the hell are you doing, Eric? You can't ask a question like that! These people are like a bunch of kids."

Eric and MB had only begun their relationship and she already knew his soft spots because Eric's left ear nearly shriv-eled up right there.

"See me right away in my office after the meeting, Eric!" she hissed.

Later, as Eric opened MB's office door, he turned towards Louise, asked her for a really big file folder favor but her phone was ringing off the hook and some kid had a bleeding nose.

* * *

What a place… it was!

Angie couldn't wait to get back to the Daycare Learning Company from her holiday and tell some of the staff at lunch that she had visited a huge Toronto store on Younge Street, which sold nothing but sex toys, skimpy underwear and videos. The store's signs were all in black and white, as if this were the only way to distinguish it from other retailers in the area. A woman clerk behind the counter had caught Angie staring at a video case and almost demanded that she ask for help before getting too carried away with the erotic pictures on the cover of the DVD container. But, Angie didn't fumble through her pockets or glance repeatedly over her shoulder because she loved being there. No, she said to herself, "Angie, you gotta feel grateful for the absence of colour here because sex is the greatest equalizer of all – even better than those tired worlds of male patronizing or sexist behaviour and some feminist movements. And movements, like some religions, don't equal-ize anything; they bully people into submission."

Anyhow, Angie will tell her co-workers at the Daycare

Learning Company to go see why this sex store should be left alone to do what it does best – celebrate sex. Like Angie said, she was not a preachy woman but this place reminded her that many people spend their entire lives becoming and being inhibited. And the only inhibiting she wanted was a pair of handcuffs on her wrists!

Wouldn't it be nice if MB came here, so to speak? Even though Angie kind of respected MB, the boss might enjoy discovering that she was not too mature to talk about sex, even to school staff. In fact, she may enjoy being in such a black and white environment. Maybe… maybe, MB might warm up and become someone else for a change.

When Angie walked into work, she thought of photocopying MB's face, attaching it to a sexy body on a door-sized poster and sending the poster to a Third World country to provide the famished with still another way of looking at hunger.

What a place… it was!

* * *

After Angie dyed her hair black, she was sometimes mistaken for one of those guerillas seen occasionally on the evening news – the same one who snarled at TV cameras when an interviewer asked about the smoking automatic rifle.

A staff member mentioned yesterday, "Hey, Angie, that long, flowing black hair and those bond paper teeth of yours make you look like MB's daughter."

"I'll take that as a compliment," was how Angie replied.

Yes, Angie admired the boss in some ways because MB could be self-righteous and heartless when she had to be, just like Angie aspired to do sometimes. Occasionally, she was even Angie's hero. Under Angie's office guise of a blouse and skirt was the green military uniform of a woman who loved ruthlessness, just like MB occasionally did. On a bad day, when Angie imagined herself as the boss, she completely forgot about holding a staff meeting but interviewed each staff member alone using a thirty-eight calibre pistol as a microphone. That… got their attention. Even old, big-hearted Irene listened carefully.

And today Grandma Irene wanted to go for a walk over lunch. "I'll buy you a chocolate bar, Angie," she said.

That Irene was the same woman who lived and breathed those so-called acts of kindness when she wasn't swooning over Chopin. Maybe, it was because she was going to retire. But Angie went out with her anyway, if only to get some fresh air.

Sure enough, Irene bought her this giant O'Henry chocolate bar at the 7-Eleven Store. Angie really didn't know how to accept this gift. People who always gave made Angie nervous. They wanted something in return, whether they admitted it or not.

"I owe you for that O'Henry bar, Irene." Angie said.

"Naw, just enjoy it, Angie and try not to figure out the reasons for giving."

Was that ever a red flag for Angie! Where had she put that microphone? Was she ever going to teach Irene about life and war once they got outside that 7-Eleven Store!

Outside, the sky darkened. Passing vehicles and pedestrians stopped moving. Angie was suddenly lost for words.

"You look like you have something important to tell me, Angie. What is it?" Irene asked.

"I'll talk to you about it later. I'm just tired. Haven't slept that well recently. Maybe, I'm watching the late news too much! In fact, I feel like I've been IN the late night news lately."

"Why is that?"

"Later, Irene."

When Angie's hair was that black, she could not sleep unless she heard shells exploding.

* * *

Even though Irene had a few freckles here and there, she somehow managed to have an all-year tan. She's always looked good at school and she worked on her skin using a special lotion and lots of time in a tanning salon. Usually, only younger staff members did this. Also, Irene spent holidays in places of perpetual sun and her few freckles were just a shade or two darker than her skin. Good thing, she didn't have lots of freckles. Otherwise, she'd probably be fair-skinned to start with and she'd be burnt from the tanning salons and the holiday sun. Irene was hooked on sun and Chopin. Each gave her a sense of well-being. Unfortunately, her face was starting to look like a brown paper bag that was left too long in a sweaty locker. However, Irene couldn't stop herself from tanning. The only time her face was momentarily tightened was when Irene flashed one of her droopy grandma grins, so she tried to snicker a lot.

MB once said: "Irene, I am amazed at how well you can talk and smile at almost the same time. Let me remind you though that we are here in school to do our teaching jobs and not to hold a bare arm next to each other and compare tans."

Ah, that poor woman! MB had black hair and dark brown

eyes but her skin was so pale, so excessive the sun wouldn't know where to start.

"Also, Irene if you think the best way to a man's heart is by looking tanned or through his stomach, then, you're aiming way too high," she said.

But Irene knew better. She knew that a woman also tried to look good to get a man and men did the same with women. And the only man MB ever had, her husband, was probably too scared to tell her the truth. Or, maybe he was in love with her white vastness.

After, Irene heard the floor creaking behind her and it was MB again.

"And one more thing, Irene – it's probably too late for a skin cancer scare but… are you planning to die as a retirement gift to yourself?"

"Ah, I see you've been taking those personality courses again," Irene snarled uncharacteristically. "You deserve a hand!"

Outside, the sun's rays encouraged gentleness.

Inside, Irene tried to clap but her hands kept missing each other.

"I didn't know you had such a nasty streak in you, Irene," MB said.

"I didn't know either," Irene replied. "I owe you so, so much!"

* * *

A couple of staff at the Daycare Learning Company told Eric yesterday: "We bet you have enough personalities inside you to fill a city."

Actually, today Eric felt like an empty, gray city next to a river because he tried to be everything for everyone around here. His Assistant Principal's job pulled his cognitive IQ down to below fifty. And he felt like he had the emotional intelligence of a twelve-year-old. Because of the sweat of his efforts and the constant boredom and pretense of administration, his clothes clung to his skin and his brain was a mud-covered street. When all of those people inside Eric worked together, he became a clown whose head was filled with a committee of fools, a committee that made the staff laugh so hard their stomachs felt tired. Outside he was funny but inside Eric was crying; he belonged in his own clown story.

Just a moment ago, Eric was sharing a table with MB in the staffroom when he told her he deserved a higher administrative position but hadn't been treated fairly by the bosses in Central Office. After all, his cousin was a boss in another office and his brother-in-law was a big boss in Central Office. After Eric asked MB to give him one reason why he hadn't been promoted, she patted him on the back, left her hand there for a second or two and then said, "Eric… Eric… I have things to do."

Eric wondered if it was because he was not that tall and his combed-back hair, on a good day, could be the colour of dark feces. He knew he could be witty and made staff laugh but his ice-blue eyes were angry. However, he would only let them cry when he was home alone. Was it also because of his small biceps? Did he have the muscle to be promoted? Eric had even lost quite a few pounds since starting this job, mostly because of the stress caused by insipid office politics. And he simply didn't know how to spread job tasks around more evenly. The last time Eric tried to escape from all this, he was at home.

There he was looking up his wife's blouse and discovering he needed sneezing powder and tweezers to see what was there, as if that had anything to do with his job. Eric's wife had more brains in her left thumb than he did between his ears.

"Why are you looking up my blouse like that, Eric?" she had asked.

"Just trying to get my mind off the job. Bear with me, will ya."

"Okay. But whatever you find, you can keep. And be hard on me will you!"

Eric loved his wife's sharp wit and she knew more about him than he did.

Yes, the Daycare Learning Company staff was probably right. There were so many people trying to get out of Eric. He became anybody if he thought it might keep individuals happy. Sometimes Eric thought of having an elevator installed from his head to his heart in order to disband that committee of jurors. Other times, he left the school at noon to buy a huge bag of wine gums so the sugar could take over and transform him into a complete twelve-year-old.

* * *

Angie was so dedicated to her job and never allowed herself to get sick at work. However, at the moment, she was shaking, sweating, and mumbling her way through a serious bout of the flu. Angie could barely stand.

"You should book off sick and go home, Angie," Louise told her.

"Angie, you look terrible," Eric mentioned about a half-hour ago.

Yet, Angie was afraid to tell MB because she would probably think Angie was putting on a show to get the rest of the day off. That was the MB's way of making things right. Angie's body trembled and she felt her bones grinding against each other. Oh no! Time to vomit again! Two staff members held Angie up by the arms and almost dragged her into the nurse's room.

"Angie, I hope you don't lose everything down the toilet bowl," someone said.

"Thanks," Angie mumbled. "I'll be okay."

Earlier, Angie's hair was like neatly crinkled straw. When she stood to splash cool water on her face, Angie looked into the mirror and saw that her straw hair was damp and stuck out all over the place, like a pile of knitting needles. Briefly studying her eyes in the bathroom mirror, Angie noticed that they brimmed with red-veined pools of desperation. Her teeth felt like they belonged in a stranger's mouth and her long neck threatened to disappear between her shoulders. Angie was a mess but she was not going home. No way!

She heard the other day from Irene that she was envied around here, that she invented the word "workaholic". Big deal! So what if she was powerless over her work and didn't know about insanity, which was doing the same thing over and over again and expecting different results. Insanity was for the insane in mental institutions. However, Angie couldn't get much done with her face in the toilet bowl. In Angie's eyes her life was certainly still manageable. Yet, all of her innards were sliding down the drain. MB was now behind her with a caring hand on her back. When she turned to look, Angie noticed MB using a few tissues to prevent the putrid smell from curling up her own nose. And Angie immediately wondered how MB learned to rehearse such humanity.

Suddenly, there was another call for Angie from the big, white telephone.

"Aaaah! I'm puking from my toes!" Angie finally exhaled.

"Want to be left alone, Angie?" MB asked, gasping. "You're much too sick for company right now."

"Don't let me keep you," Angie mumbled from inside the toilet bowl.

"You may want to think of taking the rest of the day off."

"And do what?"

Then, Angie lifted her head and the toilet flushed for the umpteenth time while she clung to the sides of the bowl, her knuckles gleaming white from all the clenching.

"Go home, Angie!" Louise pleaded. "You're crazy to stay here today!"

"Not me," said Angie, wiping vomit from her chin. "Never me."

Outside, in the hallway, the bell rang to begin Angie's afternoon.

* * *

At the staff party, Eric laughed at MB's joke mostly because he was her assistant boss but inside he knew she was so uptight he couldn't drag a needle out of her butt with a tractor.

"Eric."

"Yes?"

"What did the dry cleaner have on his window sign?"

"Drop your pants here."

"I should cuff you for that joke." I said.

"You seem to get it though."

Then Eric asked her for a slow dance and everything happened so fast. After taking a long swig from her rye and Diet Coke, she accepted his invitation and it was then that he truly realized that there was almost two of her to one of him. They danced a second slow one right afterwards and shuffled their way to a dark corner of the room. Then, Eric's mouth was on hers and their tongues sword fought with each other. For only a brief second, he worried what other staff might think. After, Eric smiled and thought of his tongue as that tractor doing such a fine job on the boss. He should be given a promotion, a raise. The song ended. And Eric now had a raise that was very hard on him. Eric's heavy breathing allowed MB and her own short breaths to take a break and walk out into the hallway away from the Home Economics room where the party was being held.

"Eric, you gotta remember that all women are gorgeous," he said to himself. "And you're gorgeous too – especially after a few drinks."

Several minutes later, after his raise vanished, MB was back and asking him for another slow dance. Soon, they were in that dark corner of the room again. Eric's raise returned and stayed for awhile. Another slow dance and they were glued to each other's bodies. Oh, she was the boss and they've both had too much to drink. That didn't stop her though because MB cajoled Eric into a darkened restroom and locked the door. Inside, she leaned against the sink and grasped him by the wrists. Then, she guided his hands around her waist and undid his belt in less time than it took her to snap open a can of pop. When his pants were down around his ankles, she went to work on him.

"Come on, Eric, lighten up!" she sighed after pulling away from him.

"Keep doing what you're doing and I really will be lighter," he gasped.

His raise was still there and it wanted to be hard on someone else besides him. But a sudden tomorrow boss thought stopped it all and he went limp when he tried to break away. MB grabbed him by the wrists again and wouldn't let go. What could he do? He tried repeating a joke she told earlier – something about two flies on a toilet seat getting pissed off. She coughed slightly then laughed again at her own joke and said, "You liked that one eh, Eric?"

Finally, Eric broke free and slipped out of her grasp. As soon as he closed the door, Eric heard the toilet flush. Right there in the hallway, he turned off his tractor and threw away the keys.

* * *

Eric knew he was only the Assistant Boss around here but why was MB so grouchy with him this morning? Was it because of what happened at yesterday's staff party? Was it because of the bits of toilet paper sticking to his face and neck from the nicks of his morning shave? Who knows? Maybe, she had that pained look because of hemorrhoids, or constipation, or a yearning to be an administrator in Central Office herself. It was intriguing to see how MB was never ever grouchy with administrators from downtown.

People in the staffroom suggested electric razors, various

razor blades and different creams for Eric's shaving. Meanwhile, he joked about anyone needing extra toilet paper to come and see him and that tomorrow, he'd come to work with the Sports Section of the Calgary Herald mapping his neck and chin. MB insisted that only she had the answer for a perfect shave and proclaimed she did her legs three times each, once a week with her Lady Schick and attained safe and perfect results.

"Can I examine one of your calves to compare it with my chin?" Eric asked.

"You serious?"

"Yes, I am."

"Not here, Eric. In my office," she whispered.

In her office, Eric stroked his chin with one hand and with the other he carefully rubbed the bottom of her calf. The beard on her leg was sparse and nowhere near the density of the hair on his chin.

"It's like comparing apples and oranges," Eric said.

"Not really. Pay attention, Eric! By the way, let's pretend that what happened at the party last night never occurred. Okay?"

"Sure."

That made it easy to pretend she was invisible. Very easy.

Then, she slammed her half-clenched fist into Eric's shoulder. He laughed so hard her fist became a bowl of spaghetti and her face an old wallet.

"Eric, let ME compare," she muttered.

"Be my guest. Have a good feel," Eric said nearly choking on his laughter.

Then, MB slipped one hand under his chin and the other caressed her calf.

"You wouldn't know the difference between sandpaper and velvet, Eric – even if your underwear were made of sandpaper, which I found out yesterday wasn't."

"You're the boss," he replied, throwing his hands up to the ceiling.

"You got that right!"

Later, as Eric rinsed out his coffee cup in the staffroom, he turned the cold water tap on all the way and watched MB slowly go down the drain, feet first. And her fingers had their own sign language when Eric offered MB a final shave.

* * *

"O Canada" became one of Eric's favorite songs.

Eric was a recently appointed Assistant Principal, a boy-man who was serious only when he was not shaking his thin bones with laughter, especially when MB tried to be funny. Because he was her only assistant boss, he made sure that he was not laughing at her but at her joke. She could tell the difference. Like this morning when Eric heard her say that whenever a woman thought she could see through a man, she was missing a lot and to remember that most men thought with their little heads instead of their big ones. The first joke Eric had heard before in an old slapstick movie from the 1940's. He said to her, "That one about seeing through people – not only is it funny, but it shows great insight on your part too!"

The second joke was about as innovative as warmed-over cabbage.

And this morning, he heard another one of her brilliant attempts when she said, "Eric you're starting to look like one of those Mexican border guards from an old Clint Eastwood film. All you need is a gold tooth and a blanket over your shoulder!"

"Bet the Mexican people would love your cultural sensitivity!" Eric replied. "So would the media."

"Oh, Eric – don't take yourself so seriously, will ya!"

Eric admitted to himself that he needed a haircut and he had this long, skimpy moustache too that could use some trimming. Recently, Eric had also been told that he carried his toughness like an invisible gun. That was just another one of his many personalities to keep the staff guessing.

At lunchtime in the staffroom, Eric pulled his huge lunch bag out of the fridge. The bag contained a one liter plastic bottle of pure orange juice, two submarine sandwiches and a plastic bag of cold cuts. Eric needed his daily fix of protein. He liked to discuss personalities because he believed his sole concern around here was the needs of others. At least, that's what he told himself. Yes, everyone behaved like they did for a reason. For example, MB pretended to be an extrovert who sensed, felt, judged and told clever jokes. For all the protein in the world, Eric never told her that but he wondered if she was nothing more than one big introvert. When he really listened to some of her jokes, Eric realized MB needed time to think them through. She was very territorial, intensive, had limited relationships and was controlling, like a few other people around here. Eric was also quite sure that she lost energy from being around people too. And she reminded him of someone who thought that any lack of impulse control or display of spontaneity was immature. Now he looked at her. Now he listened to her much more carefully.

Whenever MB was in the staffroom as the national anthem

was being played, Eric made sure he stood on guard for himself.

"O Canada" became one of Eric's favorite songs.

* * *

"You know what?" Eric asked Angie this morning.

"What?"

"Sometimes you have a heart the size of a parachute and a mind that is just as free but intensely private."

"That's quite a mouthful, Eric? Why do you say that? And what do I owe you for your incisive diagnosis?"

"I could be way off the mark but it's just something I see. And by the way, it's on the house. My dime."

"Thanks. No, you're not way off the mark. Some days it's true," Angie replied.

Angie also dreaded staff meetings and preferred to comment personally or by written means. Angie guessed that meant she was a bit of an introvert – one of Eric's favorite words that he often used to describe a few staff members.

And then she told Eric about something that happened to her when she was a little girl. "Keep this between us because if MB found out, it would be blabbed into every administrator's ear under the pretense of keeping it all within these four walls," she said.

"Just between us," Eric assured her.

"Thanks, Eric. It all may have started when I was seven years old. I was sleeping in an orphanage dorm, trying to be grateful that the institution was my parachute from my real family who couldn't take care of me anymore. At the time, both my mother and father were living their days and nights in the bottom of a beer bottle. Anyhow, just before bedtime, a nun told me if I had to get up in the night and disturb others, there was a good chance I'd go to Hell. So, I tried to slide into sleep with my bladder trembling, even though I didn't have to go pee at all. In my sleep, I saw myself urinating on the coldest of all outhouse toilet seats. When I woke up in the middle of the darkness, my sheets, blankets and mattress were soaked in pee. I spent the rest of the night trying to dry out the urine by rubbing it with my left thigh. There was no way I was going to let my parachute down. However, the smell was so bad that even a half bottle of cheap perfume made little difference. Because the powerful smells of mostly urine and some cheap perfume were still there the next morning, I caught hell from the nun. Yet, the very ugly rash on my left thigh saved me. The nun took one look at my leg and put me in the hospital. Three doctors couldn't determine how the rash was caused. Then I told them about the urine stain. I figured nothing more would happen to my parachute if I told the truth. Well, the nun thought I may have hidden emotional problems and had me talk to a counsellor. Even with all her silent nodding, you wouldn't believe how that counsellor became still another parachute for me. Anyhow, to make a long story short, I often have to fold away the parachute part of my heart today and store it away from people like MB."

"MB's not all that bad, is she?" Eric asked.

"Yea, she does have redeeming qualities so we shouldn't be so critical of her."

"Right, nobody's that wicked."

Outside, near the front entrance of the Daycare Learning

Company, a flag flapped against the steel pole, its chain clanging some uneven music.

* * *

Even at the age of thirty-two, Louise heard whispers around the school that she was still mumbling her way through puberty. Maybe, it was because she loved defying MB by wearing a suit to work one day and casual jeans the next. This drove MB crazy because of her obsession with consistency and responsibility.

Twice she had told Louise this month, "Louise, you're my secretary and you're over the age of eighteen aren't you?"

"Do I look under eighteen?" Louise asked her bottom lip curled into a snarl.

Now Louise was in the staffroom waiting by the microwave oven for her lunch of leftovers: de-boned chicken breasts with stuffed mushrooms, a crepe filled with fresh fruit and a chocolate eclair. Her husband made her lunch and knew the way to her heart! Everyone else was eating their tossed salads, their oranges and apples, their yogurt, their bowls of leftover soup. Louise felt like a cat waiting for a gourmet mouse. The humming microwave was a song, which helped her understand this staffroom of anxious waistlines pretending to enjoy the noon hour meal. Then, the microwave beeped three times. Louise's lunch was ready. She opened the door and slid her plate onto the counter. Damn! Michael, that fairly new teacher, who always bragged about making his own sandwich for lunch every day, was sitting in her chair. Louise thought of stuffing Michael's brown paper bag up his nose but re-considered.

Then, she leaned over the table and looked him straight in the eye. Louise gave him that "get your ass out of my chair" look but it did nothing.

"Out of my seat, Michael. Move!" Louise hissed.

Michael stood briefly and the two words he whispered into Louise's ear were not "fixed opinions".

Louise gritted her teeth but Michael sat down again and ignored her. Then, she decided to eat standing up right next to her chair, even though there were several other empty chairs available in the staffroom.

"Why are you eating standing up?" MB asked.

Right away, Louise whispered to herself the same two words she heard from Michael in her chair.

When MB asked Louise to repeat what she said, Louise called her a whore while pretending to clear her throat.

"Pardon me, Louise?" MB asked.

Then, Louise cleared her throat more loudly a second time.

"Awhore! Awhore! Got a frog in my throat,' Louise said.

"Sounds like something… or other is caught there."

"Exactly," said Louise

Tomorrow, Louise will wear her jeans!

* * *

Here in the Daycare Learning Company, Mick never treated colleagues in a too hot or too cold manner. He tried to keep things even and not offend anyone, if possible.

"Does this upcoming smoking ban worry you, Mick?" Eric asked him earlier today.

"Yea, Eric. I'm the grandpa on staff and I'm kind of set in my ways. You know how I love having a smoke in the staffroom before I start the day. After hearing about this ban though, I feel like some kind of gangster ready to hit the road."

And Mick loved his routines. Every day he wore the same dark brown, corduroy sports jacket, black slacks, black brogue shoes and white socks. He changed his turtleneck cotton sweater every day and of course, his socks and underwear. The only difference in colour was with his turtleneck, which could be blue, white, red, yellow or just about any other colour imaginable. This made life easier because Mick hated shopping for shirts and ties. And he preferred having root canal work done rather than ironing. Each morning, he splashed on loads of Old Spice after-shave lotion, as if it were part of his uniform. A sweet-smelling work skin.

The other day, MB said, "whenever I'm near you, Mick, that turtleneck of yours is like a blue or yellow chimney with Old Spice wafting out of it."

"Thanks! You don't smell so bad either," Mick replied. He really took MB's words as a compliment.

Mick's hair was combed back as a Duck Cut, just long enough so he could comb it over his bald spot. Hairspray kept it in all in place. Occasionally, during the evening at home, he gently touched the top of his head with a fingertip or two to check on his hair while he listened to that smooth jazz voice of Nat King Cole, the harmonies of the Everly Brothers and yes, even the Mamas and Papas. When Mick talked about his taste in music, a younger staff member asked him if any of these performers ever appeared on MUCH MUSIC and Mick forgave him for asking. The younger colleague didn't mean any harm – even though, Mick privately wondered if the colleague had the musical taste of a Smurf.

For some reason, Mick just told MB that he drank room temperature beer only and she wasn't surprised. Studying Mick, as if she had her hand moving inside his back, MB reminded him that this was how he treated staff members too – never too hot or never too cold. MB was right. Room Temperature Mick. He had to give her credit.

Mick wanted to die in the classroom with both of his brogue shoes on. He promised himself he wouldn't leave footprints on any of his co-workers, even if they stepped on him on their way up the job ladder. He imagined the paramedics carrying his chalk dust-covered body out on a stretcher and his students thinking this was just another Science experiment.

Before the staffroom chatter turned again to the smoking ban, Mick rushed to finish his cigarette. At any second, he expected MB to float back into the room, pretending to be Santa Claus but eventually wanting inoffensive Mick to be one of her elves again.

There was something in the air that was clearer than Christmas and stronger than Old Spice.

* * *

Parts of Louise were feeling older than others.

Because it was another milestone birthday for her tomorrow, Louise was sure the bottom half of her face was heading south and her waist recently developed a life of its own. The roots of her now blonde-streaked hair were showing and her distinct blue eyes were fading. Louise kept changing the colour of her hair from blonde to red to black and back again in an attempt to slow down the aging, like Eric did. At least, her cheeks were still firm, well-muscled pouches and her nose was a perfect miniature ski-jump but that was it for the youthful features. Meanwhile, the top half of her face didn't know what to do with the lower half of her face. After looking in the mirror, Louise was so uncomfortable with what she saw from the neck up that she dropped one of her contact lenses down the front of her very stylish, green dress and gasped slightly when she felt a pinch in her pubic hair. Even her capped teeth seemed painted into her mouth and belonged on the face of someone fifteen years younger.

When Louise walked out of the bathroom and got ready to go home, MB slid her hand across her shoulder and reassured her, "Louise, I'm getting longer in the tooth too. Wanna to go out for a drink after work?"

How come she knew? How did MB read Louise so well when Louise hadn't said a word yet? She must have a secret can-opener made specifically for the human head! Next time, Louise will definitely close the bathroom door all the way! She didn't like MB touching her in any way so Louise turned down her invitation saying she had an appointment to get pampered.

"Where are you going?" MB asked.

"Oh, just a little self-indulging," Louise said. "A massage. An uplifting birthday present to myself."

As Louise walked down the hallway, she asked herself what might be obtained from a coddled cow. And her answer was spoiled milk. At least, if Louise couldn't be cute, she could be clever with herself.

"Have a good massage," MB called after her. "And let me know how it went."

"Oh, I won't have to do that. You'll know!" Louise replied over her shoulder.

As soon as she stepped out the front door of the Daycare Learning Company, a five o'clock breeze caressed Louise's face and her massage began.

* * *

Actually, Jim felt that his job wasn't that special because he was needed about once a week; he came to the Daycare Learning Company on Fridays to do some testing and consulting for MB. However, Eric wanted Jim to feel like he was still part of the staff.

"Hey Jim, want to go to McDONALD'S for lunch?" Eric asked. "My treat."

At McDONALD'S, Eric casually asked why Jim didn't talk very much at work.

"Well, to tell you the truth, Eric, we really were isolated working the fields," Jim said. "I suppose we Saskatchewan farm boys did most of our gabbing at Legion Hall dances or in the Chinese Café or at Bingo."

Eric was surprised by Jim's sudden outburst and hid his awkwardness by repeatedly wiping imaginary ketchup from his moustache.

Then, for some reason or other, Jim said, "You know something Eric, I now use my bedroom mirror to get to know myself in new ways because I don't appreciate the way people like MB control the old me. She reminds me of my mother, who turns me into a boy again whenever she comes for a visit. Please don't say anything to MB! Feels like she has her hand on my back all the time at work; makes me think, talk and act the way she wants. So, I sometimes see myself as a jazz singer or a recluse comic book illustrator or a breeder of parrots instead of Jim, the Consultant. That someone else is never low-key, like I seem to be at the Daycare Learning Company. Occasionally, I see myself in a smoky bar singing like a male version of Diana Krall, dressed in black, my hair dyed blonde and my piano fingers urging love from my voice. Or, I imagine re-inventing Spiderman, and I make him a mean creep with eyes as big as dinner plates and no body bones. Or, I see myself teaching parrots to say sexy things to the owners so their hands tremble. I mean: look at me! Just look at me! I'm forty-something years old and raising my hyperactive daughter on my own. I'm all over the place! My ex-wife is too busy watching her taped re-runs of Dr. Phil to ever be a real mother. And behind my ex's pathetic self-centredness, is a mumbling, mother hen, gossip queen masquerading as a would-be poet who has the mental agility of a doorknob and the emotional development of a three-year-old. When I think of my former wife, I think of the nickname "Staller" because she lives and breathes in a procrastinator's skin. I wonder what happened to the love I had for that woman. It may have something to do with time because I see my ex constantly looking at her wristwatch, as if she were waiting to grow up. This is not nice to say but she reminds me of a dog with no legs. And where is she now, you might be thinking? Right where I left her. I'm talking too much, Eric. Not making much sense. My daughter came by her impulsivity honestly. I mean, listen to me! I better clam up."

"Wow! Never knew you had so many words inside you, Jim. Don't sweat it though! I won't say a word to anyone – especially MB."

"Thanks Eric. Recently, I've been spending less and less time in front of my bedroom mirror after shaving because consultants are constantly handing out advice.

"Has it helped, Jim?"

"Somewhat. But I hear what staffs say about consultants. Why even last week I overheard Louise say, 'Sure, sure – consultants are all talk and no walk. They know sixty ways to rob a bank but are dirt poor themselves."

On their way out of McDONALD'S Jim shoved a ten-dollar bill into Eric's back pocket.

"Lunch is on me, Eric," he said.

* * *

Irene knew she was short and she recently overheard Louise say, "That Irene is shaped like a sexy fire hydrant." Nice. Nice secretary.

At least Irene still had a shape. But she told herself, "You're okay, Irene. Your skin is still recovering from the scars of long-ago acne. That's why you love tanning so much. Remember you're the grandma on staff, so give yourself a break!"

Even still, her hair, short and mixed with dark red and gray, was matted like pillow feathers squashed by someone in the throes of one nightmare too many. But that was just hair!

Irene didn't think there was anything pretentious about herself except the way she acted around MB when they discussed Michael who had a tattoo on his forearm. She hated it when the boss talked about other staff to her. MB felt he was a hard worker and Irene thought he was a smooth-talking manipulator. Oh! Oh! There's Michael again. And for some reason, MB had Michael squirming in his shoes.

Now, he walked away from her towards Irene. Michael rolled up his sleeve. Irene couldn't believe her eyes. Finally, he was ready to show her that complete tattoo of his. Chances are he wanted something from Irene but she needed to see the entire tattoo.

"Well, well, look at that!" Irene said.

Staring her in the face was a globe of the world with the word PEACE emblazoned across the Equator.

"Hey Michael, would that world of yours want a glass of ink instead of coffee?" Irene offered.

"That's not even clever, let alone sarcastic, Irene," he said. "I've heard what Louise said about you. Maybe, you should make yourself useful and let dogs salute you with a quick lift of a paw."

"Well, Michael, I certainly wouldn't want you for my fireman and have to hook up to a hard-to-find hose like yours," Irene said.

Suddenly, MB stepped between them.

"Okay you two, that's enough!"

Then, Irene watched MB almost jabbing Michael in the chest and carrying on a one-way conversation with him while using Michael's sternum as a target. Up against a wall, his feet were ready to wiggle free from his shoes at any moment.

"Still want an ink drink, Michael? Irene asked as she left the staffroom.

"Irene, let it go!" MB commanded.

"Why?" Irene asked.

"Because I said so, that's why!" MB snarled through gritted teeth.

"Where would the Daycare Learning Company be without your astute leadership?"

"When did you say you're retiring, Irene?"

"When you go home, get on your knees and pray for brains," Irene whispered to herself.

"What was that, Irene?" MB asked. "I didn't hear you."

"When I go home, I'll gather peas and pray for rain," Irene said clearly.

* * *

Sometimes, Jim the Consultant got to listen to employee problems, except for today when he was unable to face a problem of his own.

Jim's beard was as bristly as a head of wheat and his belly, like a huge soft cushion, was tighter inside than a Boy Scout's knot. But he simply couldn't let MB find out what was wrong; she thought he was beyond any personal problems, so let her keep that illusion. And there was only one way to handle this, but Jim needed an empty office to do it.

He found a small, unoccupied room at the end of a hallway that had one desk, one chair, a small cot and one telephone; sometimes it was used as the Nurse's Room – perfect for this painful intimacy of his. Locking the small office door, he unplugged the phone and pretended there was someone he trusted sitting in the chair.

Soon, he heard himself telling the chair, "Two days ago I

mentioned to my wife that I had thoughts of being unfaithful to her. I was powerfully attracted to another woman while at a conference; however, we didn't go to bed together. We only re-created the alphabet with our tongues in each other's mouths."

Jim felt so guilty and just had to tell his spouse. Bad move. Because of his honesty, he spent the last two nights in a Super 8 Motel with a forty ouncer of Captain Morgan White Rum next to his bed. Jim desperately wanted to move back home with his wife and kids but he was obsessed with guilt.

Then, he sobbed at the empty chair, but the tears weren't effective. The chair was at first sympathetic but then became distant. Later, Jim swore he heard the chair giving him a bit of advice. Something about him taking ownership of the problem – whatever that really meant. Knowing full well that Jim had used those words on colleagues, he thought of how MB used the same language at staff meetings and the words tasted like re-heated coffee. And at the moment, a similar message was coming back to Jim from an empty chair. Well… it reminded him of any consultant, who was basically a pickpocket stealing a wallet and then offering to lend the victim money from the same wallet.

Oh! Oh! Someone was at the door. It might be MB. Jim opened the door and it was her! MB took one look and knew immediately that something was upsetting him. Jim waited for her to calmly sweep away any possible intimacy with the fleshy broom of her tongue.

Instead, MB said, "Jim… you're needed… really needed… at the office."

* * *

Without thinking twice one day, MB said, "You know something, Louise? Maybe that mentally handicapped son of yours makes you work harder at losing your mind."

"What are you talking about?" Louise replied. "I may be only the secretary around here but I know stupidity when I hear it!"

"Don't take it so personally, Louise."

"He's my son. How can I NOT take it personally?"

"I only meant that having such an emotional investment in someone like your son and not being able to do much about it could make anyone crazy."

What kind of a moronic crack was that? Why couldn't MB just mind her own business, keep her mouth shut and do what was in front of her? Simple but effective.

Louise realized that for quite a few years, she denied that her son was handicapped but today she fully accepted his condition. She still contended that his mind was frequently sharper than hers. And she had heard whispers in the Daycare Learning Company that she was becoming a lot like her mentally handicapped son. However, Louise knew that she had absolutely no control over how other people thought, felt or acted, so what they said about her was none of her business.

All she knew was that her son predicted before she did when she was in a reflective mood – like right now as she was drinking a cup of water. Louise was sure he knew she was sipping water at this time and flashing her happy, morning, quarter-moon smile at the world. Then, Louise opened the tap and poured herself a second cup of cold water. As she tipped the paper cup to her mouth, droplets of cool water trickled down her chin. Just as the first few drops hit the floor, Louise flashed her chalk-white teeth at the reflection of herself in the teakettle. Next, she heard her son's thoughts and they were telling his mother he would kill for her and that her pensive attitude was healthy. At the bottom of the water cooler, Louise saw something twitching and it was a nervous wreck that was formerly her.

Moments later, MB stood directly behind Louise fluttering her eyelashes, like tiny flags and she reminded Louise that she had another significant idea ready to be launched into the staffroom.

"So, what's so deep about your thinking now?" Louise asked her.

"I just had another incredible notion about your son."

"And what would that be?"

"Later, Louise; this one is beyond both of us."

"Try it out on me anyway, will ya."

MB fell silent.

Shortly after, she imagined MB as a mannequin in a window of a Bay department store. Louise felt her fingers dressing the dummy but nothing fit properly. Then, she plopped the MB nudity on her lap and Louise held her like a helpless, oversized puppet. The first thing Louise did was to give the MB mannequin a severe speech impediment. And she was about to wish more on the mannequin but the staffroom door squeaked open and the room filled with co-workers. As she walked by Louise, MB whispered, "Louise, did you know that your mind can do whatever it wants?"

"That's profound," Louise replied. "Quite profound but... what about my son?"

* * *

The early morning for Angie's husband was a time when he ran into a concrete wall.

"So, does that mean he's grouchy when he first gets up, Angie?" someone asked.

"Yea, I think it's mostly because he has to get up extra early for his shift as an Air Canada baggage handler at the airport."

"Must be tough on you waking up to that kind of stuff everyday," someone else said.

"Actually, I look forward to it. It's like an eye-opening show for me."

Angie liked to entertain the staff by imitating her man's foul, early morning disposition. The staffroom always felt lighter afterwards. She never did this in front of MB though because she once took Angie aside and said that it wasn't professional office behaviour. Sometimes, Angie felt that MB's maturity looked and felt like a wrinkled prune.

Anyhow, the boss was away this morning so Angie could cut loose all she wanted. And today, she was just bursting with trouble. Angie made her face lopsided and pretended to be shaving. Next, she hiked her eyebrows and stretched her forehead and nose while pretending to get dressed. Then, Angie puffed her cheeks in and out while eating a fake breakfast of toast and cereal. After, she twisted and turned her mouth while brushing her teeth and grumbled her way around the staffroom. Later, Angie shrugged her shoulders up and down, as if she were about to be stretched on a rack. As she pretended to be putting on her coat to leave for the airport, Angie turned her head back and forth and mumbled how badly the world treated her. Each of her facial contortions and body movements became airport baggage crawling down the chute onto a carousel.

"Pretend you are waiting for baggage," Louise said to the staff. "Think of my husband's early morning moods, like so many different suitcases sliding down the chute onto a conveyor belt. Ready?"

And she watched as colleagues gathered around a coffee table in the staffroom pretending it was a luggage carousel. Meanwhile, after each bad mood husband face, Angie relaxed her skin and pretended that she was the picture of serenity. Co-workers looked from Angie to the coffee table and back again. And they howled with laughter while flinging imaginary suitcases: on top of the coat rack, into garbage cans, onto the floor, into the sink, onto the couch, into the microwave oven, out the window, into cupboards, onto the stove, into the fridge, even out the window – anywhere and everywhere.

When the staff was all laughed out, Angie proclaimed, "Tomorrow morning, I will remind that spouse of mine that whenever he runs into a concrete wall, he should learn to say 'damn'."

"When you tell him that, don't be too hard on yourself," Irene said, bringing her hand to her mouth to hide her laughter.

"And please tell your husband to get off that rack of his, will you!" Louise shouted looking around at everyone. "We need the screws!"

* * *

Occasionally, Irene was told she looked like the photograph of MB's long lost, older cousin found in the boss's office.

Irene hoped they didn't think she was anything like MB though because she hated any of those boss thoughts in her life. She was just here to eat her lunch and finish off her career – one day at a time. You know the usual – keep her mouth shut, mind her own business and just do what was in front of her. At this stage in Irene's life, the fewer doors opened, the better.

First, she very systematically wiped a spot at the table with a lace handkerchief from her purse. Next, Irene laid her wrinkle-free, brown cloth bag directly in front of her on the table. After, she gently reached into the bag and withdrew a single sandwich without once touching the inside of the bag. Then, with the fingers of a concert pianist, Irene used only the thumb and forefinger of each hand to unfold the wax paper from the sandwich. The crustless tuna sandwich was gently placed on a plate, as if she were offering it to her own God; she owed everything to the good, orderly direction in her life. Folding the wax paper neatly back on itself, Irene slipped it into the bag, again without touching the inside of the bag. The bag was then gently folded into its own, natural creases and left on the table to the exact left of her plate. Soon, she used the same thumb and forefinger and aimed the sandwich towards her mouth. Her lips barely moistened the bread as it slipped into her mouth. Irene didn't chew; she massaged her food. After the sandwich bite was moistened just enough, it barely slid down her throat unnoticeably, like oxygen.

By the way, MB did not teach her how to eat. Irene was not her sister. Besides, after she drank her Diet Coke and swallowed the last of her Cherry Blossom chocolate bar alone in her office, Irene's non-sister rehearsed such sanctimonious proclamations as:

"Irene, Irene, you need to lighten up. You're going to retire soon and for every stressful year you have now, you shave two off the other end!"

And that fake compassion was exactly what kept Irene away from MB.

Outside the staffroom window, Irene watched a sparrow on a tree branch clear its throat in the sunshine and she took a wild guess at how many years the bird had left.

* * *

I heard what that teacher said about me.

"That Jim may be our consultant but he's also a neurotic weasel who probably lifts weights and takes secret boxing lessons and nothing more. And when he wears that black leather jacket of his to the Daycare Learning Company, he looks like an undercover narcotics agent."

But all I said was that there can be no slowing me down. My job owned me. The wheels that supported my dedication will never sink into the ground, like jam. Although I never allowed that to happen, I'm still human enough and I practiced by treating myself to a cabbage roll or two every Friday night. And lots of people around here appreciated me because they said I did the work of three people, even though I could tell they wanted as little social contact with me as possible.

Oh, oh, there's Angie. Bet she needs some more of my guidance.

"Angie, I hear that MB wants you to shape up. Do you think that's a fair assessment?" Angie did not answer and her mouth shaped two words that were inappropriate for the Daycare Learning Company. If she said those words to MB, her fat, young butt would be in a sling. Occasionally, I wondered if Angie suffered from the affects of wearing her underwear too tight.

I knew my hair was turning gray and if my lips were any thinner, they'd disappear into my face but I felt I moved and breathed like a sixteen-year-old. My older brother, who was a doctor, said that even a sixteen-year-old needed to rest sometimes. Yet, I downhill skied every weekend and I kept up with a lot of those young ones. I even ate animal cookies for dessert. My energy ate the giraffe and elephant cookies bobbing over my lunch bag everyday. I thought that was funny.

I hadn't told anyone at the Daycare Learning Company about my drinking though. They wouldn't understand why last weekend I went to a church across the street, filled an empty Diet Coke can with holy water, slipped it into my pocket and then went home. Why? So I could guzzle down all that holy water before I opened my bottle of white rum. That way, I figured God might protect me from getting too drunk.

Oh, oh, Angie was coming towards me again. Her teeth looked as if they were grinding the distance between us. She carried a bunch of folders and was reading the top one. What did she want now? Maybe, she needed me to write a reference letter for her. She required it very soon if she didn't improve her job performance. Her stiff walk told me her underwear had tightened even more as I spoke.

Maybe, we should go skiing together this Saturday. And then again, maybe we shouldn't.

* * *

Although I don't spend too much time in front of a mirror, I noticed today that my face was surrounded by thick, bushy curls and was sliced up by so many frowns, a cartographer could include my photograph in a geography textbook. Why was life chopping me up into pieces like this? Ah, what was I doing standing in front of the mirror when I was here for kids and kids only?

My husband said just last weekend that I'm forever gargling with joy but never swallowing it.

"Instead of just enduring life, when are you ever going to enjoy it?" he asked.

"When you stop measuring my frowns," I replied.

And I always thought the school was the only place where I rehearsed my scowling, which may be one of the reasons staff members called me MB or Missionary Boss behind my back.

Oh, there's that mother whose daughter used to attend this school. I remember how the same mother was quite rough around the edges but was very happy with how her little girl did in Grade Five. But what's she doing here? Her kid didn't attend this school anymore. And was the woman ever losing her hair! Wow! I better keep my eyes away from her receding hairline. Strangely enough, I had to say little to her but I was fascinated by her hair loss as she got closer and closer to me.

"Want to rub my forehead? You look curious," she said.

She knew what I was thinking. How come? Where were my frown lines?

"Well I… . By the way, how's your daughter doing in her new school?"

"Come on, what you really want to do is give my thinning hair a little pat and not ask about my daughter," she said.

Trying desperately to untie my tongue, I dropped my head to my chest.

"Come on, massage my forehead, will you. It feels like my husband's butt, you know."

And the mother laughed so loudly, the floor tiles beneath our feet vibrated.

My head turned this way and that, looking for my frown lines. Oh, there they were, lying on the floor, like lost knitting needles.

"Excuse me for a moment, I have an office matter to take care of," I told the mother. "I'll be right back."

"Did you just lose something?" she asked me with a mischievous look on her face. "Like your touch. I'm only here to visit."

"The office matter can wait!" I said as I turned and walked back towards her high forehead.

* * *

Around here, I was the union rep even though I was the grandma on staff and not far away from retirement. I only worked part-time for MB in the Daycare Learning Company. The other half of my job was strictly union business.

I wasn't sure what was bothering Eric. He must be in a bad mood or something because he just said, "Irene, your mouth is the same size as that vast arid region between your ears."

"Eric, what did I do to deserve that? How about I introduce your teeth to your nose?" I answered.

"You better not or I will launch a union grievance against you," he said. "And you the union rep! Ha!"

"You should try launching a grievance against yourself," I said with a slight grin on my face. "You'd lose, no matter what!"

"Nothing retiring about you, Irene," he said.

"Think I'll postpone retirement just to be around you, Eric!"

Eric was supposed to be some kind of a leader around here. After all, he was the Assistant Principal! Maybe he thought I didn't have a sense of humor but Eric didn't know rights from lefts and couldn't find his ass with both hands. I wished his mother had taken The Pill or at least taught Eric that he couldn't treat employees like moronic plebeians when he got into his moods.

There's MB's voice over the intercom and her words were directed at Eric, "Please see me in the Main Office, right away!"

Then, Eric about-faced his way down the hall, as if he were readying himself for military training.

Even though he had left, my fists were whiter than white. Because of his insult, Eric was now living rent-free inside me. I once heard that I should pray for people like Eric but I couldn't think of an idiot prayer as the words were locked behind my clenched teeth. The tension was greater than an uncooked length of spaghetti noodle but Eric was out of the room at least. So, I thought of him as the only man to get pregnant with his first child and that this time, his better half didn't even wake him up. That thought made me feel better and only then could I pray for him.

However, the next time Eric got nasty, I told him that the reason gorillas have big nostrils was because they have big fingers. After he grunted at me, I prayed he was capable of picking a winner.

* * *

She couldn't wait to be a school administrator.

Whatever Angie needed to do around here to get things done her way, she did, like a few months ago when she literally pushed the Music Teacher into changing the seating plan at the Christmas concert. Another time she forced a student to change his mind about being picked on by another boy so she could prove a colleague was wrong. It was either Angie's way or the highway. Her ego was as tall as she was short! And MB didn't care because Angie was doing some of MB's job for her.

"Angie, do whatever you think will improve this school," MB once said.

Angie came from Vancouver but originally from Gibraltar. She had asthma and didn't sleep very well. Not many people around here respected her except for two Kindergarten teachers who weren't very bright and were afraid of her. Angie even had these two women wearing the same kind of black winter coat as hers. One of them cleaned up Angie's classroom for her last June because Angie's father died the second last day of school and Angie was in charge of all funeral arrangements.

Last winter, Angie took a kick boxing course because she couldn't predict when she'd have to be a Charlie's Angel. Actually, she felt like one walking heavily down the hall in her

Made in Canada black boots. If she had to, Angie tried to force the younger staff to respect her and sometimes her actions blew up in her face – like two days ago when someone her age told her to "flock off back to Gibraltar". Too bad experienced teachers either ignored her or laughed at her. They say that Angie was a sick woman who needed some serious help. She dismissed their comments saying that those oldies wouldn't be around the Daycare Learning Company much longer.

Angie's father just died last year at forty-nine years of age. Did he ever love listening to The Rolling Stones. He'd have their music cranked up really loud when she came home after school. Yet, he and Angie's mother were still talking about separating just days before his death so she said little about their relationship, as if it were the secret behind her scowl.

According to Angie, her younger sister was so self-centred because the sister was planning a trip to Italy this summer with her mother, who had been too busy feeling sorry for herself after her husband's death.

And the sixteen-year-old baby brother, well… Angie had to be his real mom and made sure he got good marks in high school or she'd snarl him down to size.

Angie hated hugs. When she was a little girl, she had aunts and uncles constantly hugging and kissing her. But her parents always asked Angie for her thoughts on everything from paying the bills to deciding on punishment for Angie's younger sister and brother. Angie's opinion was that important!

And Angie just got married last Christmas to a man who was the perfect puppy dog.

Wow, she just got word. Next year, Angie was going to be an Assistant Principal in another school. And what was this other sheet doing in her mailbox? It was a Code of Conduct Report signed by seven teachers. It stated quite clearly that Angie was a control freak bully, a "chicken with no bite" and a copy of the report would be sent to all staff at her new school.

Angie really loved dogs though because they only wanted to please her.

* * *

"Why can't you leave MB at work, Louise?" I sometimes asked myself.

It's been hell on a string since I found out that my husband had a brain tumor. And to top it all off, we're still getting used to our newly adopted nine-year-old son. Just last night my husband and I took the boy out for Chinese food and later to hear the Calgary Symphony Orchestra. I mean the kid came from an aboriginal background and here we were forcing him to be white with Chinese food and classical music. Anyhow, at the restaurant, we tried to be like one of those TV families – you know, reminding the boy about good table manners, being patient, gentle – but nothing worked. The kid hated the rice, the noodles and egg rolls, which he called cat food. The more my husband and I sampled various dishes, the more our son meowed. It was awful! And I could see my husband rubbing his forehead harder and harder as the meowing got louder and louder. For a brief moment, I thought his head would burst until he leaped out of his seat grabbed our son by the collar, and shook the kid until he stopped meowing. When the waitress came over to ask if our meal was fine, I ordered a hamburger for my son. That did it and we finished the rest of our meal in peace. But that was only supper. We still had to go to the symphony. I didn't want to waste those three tickets, although I had this tight, impending sense of doom behind my ribs.

At the concert, the first selection from Bach, called Brandenburg Concerto Number One, was being played for no more than thirty seconds, when our boy began squirming wildly in his seat. Said he hated elevator music because it reminded him of going to the dentist on the seventh floor of a tall building. We left after that first Bach piece.

On the way home, all I thought of was MB for some reason. I heard her omniscient solutions to every life problem at the Daycare Learning Company. She would have made it a point to express heartfelt sympathy for my husband's condition, as if only her words made the possible brain tumor disappear. And she'd send our boy back to the Reserve in a Baroque second.

When we got home, my husband took out his stopwatch, massaged the left side of his head and timed our son to get into his pajamas. The ticking got louder and louder. I watched him tap his thigh in unison with the ticking stopwatch. When my husband ran out of seconds, he leapt out of his chair and stormed into our son's bedroom.

"Louise, Louise... you gotta leave those boss thoughts at work!" I heard myself say just as my husband exploded.

II

BULLETS AND BRAINS

"Michael, Michael… you need more teeth to handle MB," I said to myself.

I know. I know. She recently said I take too much ownership for the floors of the Daycare Learning Company. She loves that word "ownership". All this because I keep my classroom so squeaky clean.

Some staff call me The Big Olive behind my back because I'm part Italian and a bit overweight. But this morning I was so, so proud of my cleaning and polishing job that I couldn't care less what they said. If no one walked on my floors ever again, I'd eat off them. I know. I know. It's the caretaker's job to wash and wax the floors and not mine. But, I've wanted to be a simple caretaker all my life and this was a special floor day. After our real caretaker washed and waxed the floors, I re-did my classroom floor and the floor in the hallway just outside my room.

"What are you doing, Michael? I just washed and waxed that floor yesterday after school!" the Caretaker said.

"They are my floors too!" I said.

"Are you nuts?"

"Do crazy people worry about floors?"

"Just you, Michael. Just you."

After all, my classroom is right by the front entrance. It's gotta look beautiful, just beautiful!

After I licked my chipped front tooth and grinned, I asked the teachers to come in by the back entrance and remove their shoes too. They all complied. However, MB was the last one to arrive today and head-bowed, she trundled straight into me at the front entrance. The motor of her purple Buick was still running outside the front door.

"Michael, all floors are meant to be walked on," she reminded me.

Then that word "ownership" slipped from her mouth again and I immediately thought of stuffing the Caretaker's floor polisher up her butt. You know – give her a good, Big Olive shine. Almost immediately, she pushed her way past me to her office.

"Why are you being so silly about floors, Michael?" she snarled.

What a nerve! All my life I craved for a perfect floor. Today that happened.

Seconds later, the boss returned, her black coat still buttoned up, and brushed by me with several folders in one hand and a bursting briefcase in the other. I watched her unlock her Buick and slide into the front seat, dumping both her briefcase and folders on the seat beside her. She looked straight through me. I studied her fingers tabulating her choices in the steering wheel grooves. What was she going to do about my floors and me?

When I first came here, MB admired the way I almost treated each floor, like a lover. More recently though, she became more irritable and really reminded me of my wife.

Last night in bed, my wife said that we used to hold hands, so I leaned over and held her hand. Then, she said we used to hug so I wrapped my arms around her. After, she told me I used to nibble on her neck so I got out of bed and went to the bathroom to get my partial dentures.

I needed more teeth for the boss.

* * *

"Angie, with those huge eyes of yours, there are days when you could be a double for a young Joan Collins," Louise said to me yesterday.

"I'll take that as a compliment," I replied. "Thank you!"

I often dyed my hair or changed my hairstyle. Today, it was long, shiny and draped over my shoulders, like a small black cape. According to some people, my smile resembled a youthful Joan Collins but I was not her. Sure, I loved to have Joan's money; maybe her men too. And even though I didn't quite recall seeing pictures of a young Joan Collins, I enjoyed what Louise said anyway.

The other day, a colleague accidentally overheard that MB wanted to nominate me for both a teaching excellence award and an acting award, mostly because of my dignity and the way I behaved like a twenty-year veteran around here when in fact, I was fairly new in this business. "We should call it the Joan Collins Award," someone said.

The colleague mentioned that everyone noticed the cool,

calm way, for example: the way I took my paycheque from the boss, snapped open my purse in one smooth motion and slipped in the envelope. Was Joan Collins that slick?

My man sometimes remodeled kitchens. He said I'm smoother than any kitchen counter he has built. But I wished he lightened up more, just like I wanted the boss to relax more. I wanted my man to laugh at my dirty jokes, the same jokes I wished I told MB. Forget about being smooth. Tell me the one about the farmer's son and the duck. You know – what the farmer's son tried to exchange for his bird. Rhymes with duck. Secretly, I adored dirty jokes. Because I tried so hard not to tell any raunchy ones at work, people maybe think that I'm somewhat reserved.

If only they knew how many times I imagined each and every one of them with at least one duck in their arms. And if they saw my lacey, black underwear, they'd clasp their mouths with their hands and automatically, I'd be made a movie star such as Joan Collins.

"Angie. Angie. I never knew you were the type who wore underwear like that," a couple of staff might say.

"There are lots of things you don't know about me," I'd reply.

"Really?"

"Really."

Perhaps, I need to have my own reality TV show so I could give everyone at the Daycare Learning Company all the ducks they wanted!

* * *

Once I was in love with a SAFEWAY produce clerk and it was hard to concentrate on work. A few people at the Daycare Learning Company wouldn't leave me alone.

"Angie. Does he work in fruits or vegetables or is he not sure yet?" they teased.

They all knew. Even MB exhaled loudly and wished that I concentrated on how I earned my paycheque around here. Bet she wanted me to take an unspecified day off and just go home. A couple of guys in particular teased me about my lover's melons, pears, tomatoes, prunes and his freshness – especially after the produce clerk's singing telegram and a dozen yellow roses arrived at the school for me. After the messenger left, the men did their own singing telegram in dreadful falsettos. And my laughter caused the fragrance from the flowers on my desk to tremble their smells all over the place. Meanwhile, the boss sipped from her can of Diet Coke watching me shoo away co-workers so I could get some work done. I could almost hear her sermon about leaving love stories at home.

"Tell us, Angie. Tell us all about HIS seeds, his cores, the roots and husks of his masculinity," one of the guys continued. "And when you peeled away his manhood, what did you find, Angie?"

I begged them to stop their teasing and they tried to be good. But, I was fresh material for the boys, and they only let up when MB told them they'd better stop or she'd use their jokes for fertilizer in her paper garden.

"Is that a funny place?" one of the men asked MB."

"And what kind of vegetables do YOU grow?" Angie inquired.

"The kind that are best eaten raw," MB replied with a growl.

"Ever been in love?" Michael asked.

"And why would you ask that, Michael?"

"Take a guess," he replied. "It has nothing to do with work."

"Ah, Michael, I can't keep up with your clever mind," MB said while throwing both hands into the air.

And right after Angie gave Michael a huge hug in front of everyone, Michael said to MB, "Gee, thanks Boss."

"No problem, Michael. Same with you, Angie. By the way, my garden is your garden – anytime."

"Much appreciated," said Angie.

"I'm overwhelmed," said Michael.

* * *

Recently, I said to Eric, "I challenge you to a water pistol duel in one week."

"Are you serious, Irene? A geezer like you challenging ME to a water fight?" he said.

"Eric, I suggest you go into training first so you can keep up with this geezer! One week from today, meet me in the parking lot."

"You're on, Irene, but be sure to take your geezer pills first."

"Why?"

"Because I've noticed recently that you're having trouble with such things as numbers."

"What are you talking about, Eric?"

"Numbers. Counting."

"What numbers?"

"Irene, every time you count, you always choke on that last number before seventy."

"You better start taking pills too, Eric. And keep taking them until I tell you to stop!"

The next morning I slipped a plastic, light green water pistol into Eric's mail-slot so he knew I meant business. I was very, very curious about Eric, even though his humor was occasionally tasteless. On the odd occasion, he had a spirituality about him that could make some clergymen seem like burnt-out magicians. And I asked myself about the relationship between spirituality and a water pistol duel between consenting adults. I laughed aloud about the possibilities.

During the next several days, Eric and I teased each other about our upcoming duel, which was to take place outside the Daycare Learning Company parking lot on the last day of school.

"Eric, remember to wear your rust proof clothing," I said. "Your body parts will be squeaking by the time I get finished with you!"

Unfortunately, MB overheard and reminded us we are both adults, that we should restrict our squirting antics to anywhere but the Daycare Learning Company property.

"Right," I said.

"Sure. Easy does it," the spiritual side of Eric said.

On the day of the duel, we met in the parking lot and co-workers watched from behind closed windows. We chased, pointed and squirted each other. Then, we retreated. Soon we chased again and pointed and squirted, as if our lives were at risk. Then, we retreated again laughing so hard that the one cloud in the sky shook. And we chased each other over and over while pointing and squirting. Laughing the years off our bones, we squirted again and again until we ran out of water. Panting, exhausted, and soaking wet, we looked at each other with a new belief.

"You're pretty quick for a geezer, Irene," Eric said.

"Had enough, Eric? Need to go inside for a nap?" I asked.

Then, we dragged ourselves into the Daycare Learning Company, gasping our happiness, like two kids. In the staff-room, we filled our guns again. Waiting patiently outside MB's closed door, we became very serious. We provided each other with almost God-like reasons for melting the ice cubes in MB's pants and then soaking her with our joy.

"I'll pray for her," Eric said.

"We could have a long wait before your prayers are answered," I added.

"Not really," Eric said. "Watch this."

* * *

"Irene, you just love being outside, don't you?" Eric said the other day. "You look like you belong there all the time – especially after the way you enjoyed our water pistol fight."

I knew some people made fun of me behind my back. Once, I overheard someone saying that I looked like a GREYHOUND bus because I was in love with a GREYHOUND bus driver. That wasn't funny, not funny at all. Actually, I privately wished I looked like the greyhound dog instead.

Ever since my first husband died, I've felt as if I could outlive ten men, including my current boyfriend. There was something true about men being weak, maybe because of that XY chromosome. But, at least they had something to love! And everyone knew how I felt about men. Sure couldn't keep any secrets around here!

I power-walk to work everyday trying to shed some of my extra pounds. My hair was graying but my cheeks often felt as red as suddenly lighted embers because I thrived in the outdoors. Inhaling as much fresh air as possible, I tried to protect myself from that over-sized farm nose of MB. I also required some extra energy to handle the union representative job.

On weekends, I accompanied my boyfriend on his GREYHOUND bus route and sat on a front seat next to him. Yet, sometimes during those weekend trips, I feel cooped up in the bus but I want to be near my man at any cost. If I feel my face sagging and losing its colour, I imagine myself outside walking or hiking somewhere. However, the fresh air has to wait until we stop for a meal break because windows can't be opened in this air-conditioned vehicle.

Last Sunday night, after I returned from another quick GREYHOUND trip, I found a message on my answering machine from MB. I also heard her nose rubbing against the receiver as she said she'd like to see me first thing tomorrow morning – something about a conference budget change. This could have waited until I got to work.

I hung up the phone and unplugged everything. Then, I heaved open a window and sucked in air, like a greedy geezer. My lungs felt like my XX chromosomes were inviting me to stand tall and straight in the night. Unlike most men, who were like perpetual cubs, I had no desire to roll over on my back and have my belly scratched.

Suddenly, there was a knock at the door and it was my boyfriend.

"Did you forget something on my bus?" he asked in his most professional bus driver voice.

* * *

My anger came first.

Everything else, including physical, emotional, intellectual and spiritual growth came second. Maybe, it was because I'm Mick, the oldest guy on staff and my wrath started so long ago. I am even older than Irene. They'll have to carry me out of the Daycare Learning Company in a coffin because I refused to retire and be home alone with that angry self.

The other day I blamed it all on my alcoholic mother; everything I did at home or at school was never quite good enough. I never washed the right way or dressed well enough. My marks in school were rarely high enough. I lived with the noose of perfectionism around my neck – sometimes tight and sometimes not, but always there. Occasionally, I wanted to cross that bridge of forgiveness but the bridge was too high.

At lunch today, Eric was uncharacteristically mean for some reason and blurted out, "Mick you should go home, get on your knees and ask for wisdom before you go to bed."

Just like that, Eric became MB's nasty assistant. Everyone, including MB, snickered and stared in shock first at me and then Eric. The staff was trying to work on self-esteem for several weeks and now Eric had blown it. All staff eyes were focused on me as they watched my resentment go through another silent developmental stage. Then, I walked slowly towards the refrigerator, opened the door with knuckles whiter than the appliance itself, took out my unsweetened grapefruit juice, a tray of ice cubes and poured myself a tall one. The room was so quiet the refrigerator motor sounded like a tank grinding its way through the staffroom. Eric remained absolutely silent. I felt the other staff members studying me closely and watching me smack my lips with more and more intensity, as if I were about to eat an entire grapefruit. I could actually hear Eric fastening his imaginary seatbelt and feel his growing fear. Then, I saw him taking the psycho path through an open field by moving backwards towards the staffroom door. I loaded my invisible gun. Finally removing my noose, I paused, cocked the gun and took aim. Ice cubes could be heard creaking on the counter. And just before Eric backed through the doorway, I watched MB collecting more bullet shells than brains on the staffroom floor.

My anger came first.

* * *

I always bought my husband's clothes because he needed a boss at home and I was it. He hadn't a clue about things like shoes, socks and underwear. Being a few years older than him, I thought he married me to be his mother, so maybe I was that typical older wife and maybe I wasn't. All I knew was that I was the boss at the end of the day too.

He worked as an assistant boss in another Daycare Learning Company branch and he insisted on looking the part. Calling me his snappy dresser assistant, my man said I did a much better job than he or his own mother ever did. No more needed to be said. I was quite accepting about buying his pants in particular.

He bought the groceries every week and did the laundry and vacuuming each Sunday, so I didn't have to do everything.

Oh, have I told you about the latest bargains in men's shirts and especially pants? Boy, I knew pants! In three seconds, I could tell by the crotch if the pants fitted my husband. He needed lots of room down there, if you get what I mean. I was filling in for his mother but we had a life between the sheets too, you know.

Oh! Oh! I forgot. I was still here at the Daycare Learning Company and the staff meeting was about to begin. I cleared my throat at the staffroom door. Then, I heard myself breathing mechanically through my nose, as if I were priming my brain for today's meeting agenda. Eric handed me a cold can of Diet Coke and I snapped open the tab. "Okay everyone, let's get this meeting started," I said.

Then, I reminded everyone about who wore the pants around the Daycare Learning Company: my pants, Eric's pants, Michael's pants, Mick's pants, Angie's pants – all the pants that were mine to wear, whether anyone liked it or not.

"Anyone got a problem with that?" I asked.

"Not me," said Eric.

"Not me," said Michael.

"Not me," said Mick.

"I might," said Angie.

"Eric, get me another Diet Coke," I said.

"Ask Angie," Eric said. "She MIGHT."

"I'm not asking Angie. I'm asking you."

"What have you got in your pants today, Eric?" asked Angie.

* * *

Around here, everyone called her Single Issue because she was the Daycare Learning Company Librarian, cared only about books and preferred being alone most times. For some reason or other I felt like she was living part of my life for me.

At lunch, she went for walks by herself or with one of the other loners on staff. When Single Issue was around other people, she lost energy. There was far more to Single Issue than met the eye.

And I realized all this as the boss (or MB behind my back) – especially when she noticed me entering the library. I caught her talking intensely to another staff member. The conversation stopped abruptly when I approached the main desk.

"Don't let me interrupt," I said.

"Oh, you're not interrupting. We just finished our conversation," Single Issue said.

Last week I inadvertently told Eric that she looked like one of the teddy bears she kept on the top shelves of her bookcases. I used the words "short", "fluffy" and having a "permanent grin".

"Your stuffed animals bring a warm, personal touch to the library," I told Single Issue. And I meant what I said.

Today, when Eric and I walked into the library, the books needing to be catalogued were stacked this high on her desk. Nobody was there and we couldn't see Single Issue behind her books. Without thinking Eric said, "Bet our librarian is trying to prolong her own childhood with those teddy bears. But… pretend you never heard me say that."

Out of the corner of my eye, I saw Single Issue lowering

her fluffy brown hair behind her desk as I felt her juices being sucked dry by Eric's comments. However, I didn't tell Eric.

Hearing even more Eric insights about such things as Single Issue's half-moon smile, I imagined her ducking further below her desk and writing Eric a letter about who she was. In her letter she told him how she may be quiet because her thinking worked best when turned inward. Keeping her emotions private was vital to her. Embracing privacy and shunning interruption, her letter reminded Eric that she was born to spend time alone, although it was so ironic how she ended up as a Librarian. Preferring to learn by checking the Internet or other research sources, she avoided just asking someone for information. Her letter also said that she was creative – particularly with stuffed animals, shy and required time to think about a problem and get back with a response after a meeting. And she asked when Eric will learn that she depended mainly on herself and not only on teddy bears to satisfy her own needs. After all, Eric should understand as he was the one who often used the word "introvert" around the Daycare Learning Company. And the last line in her letter stated that her teddy bear behaviour was her reality and not her excuse, her issue and not Eric's.

Sometimes, at home, when I was not MB or the boss, I felt exactly like Single Issue and those feelings remained as seldom-worn blouses in my closet.

* * *

That Eric! I mean he was just another pecker who thought he could slowly seduce any woman on staff just like that. Well, I may be only the secretary around here but did I have news for him!

And when I looked in the bathroom mirror, I saw that my eyes were raging above my no-chin. I once heard Eric suggest to another male colleague that I should be handed a fork and knife so I could eat my lunch lying on my back from my flat-as-a plate chest. Nice guy. I should have complained to MB but she would have said, "Louise, don't take Eric so seriously! And why don't you just go to your doctor and ask for a prescription of you-know-what pills. That'll help."

She had an answer for everything.

Then, I turned and the image in the mirror showed that I have quite the sexy butt – cupped, round and firm. My husband said it was breathtaking and that certainly was good enough for me. But Eric never asked me about equality in bed because my husband was head and shoulders taller than he could ever be. No, the action in my bed was just fine thank you. And if Eric ever tried to put a serious move on me, my husband would introduce his ribs to his teeth.

Wait a minute. What's that? I'll cup my ear to the door. Eric was talking about me in the other room. Yea, he was saying nasty things about me.

"I'd like to wrap some electrical tape around her beak just to shut her up for eight hours. Get MB to hire someone else for the day. Wouldn't it be nice? Then we could…"

I'll wait. I'll wait until he's finished his yammering and then burst into the room. Then, I'll inform him, in no uncertain terms, about real frostbite or what happened when you crossed a frozen beak with a pecker.

Outside, a jackhammer punched the sidewalk silly as the sun grew up the sky.

* * *

"You know something, Louise? You have hidden talents," MB said. "And I need you to work with Eric to get a bunch of paperwork done for me. I'm way behind on a project."

"I'm not so sure about working with Eric," I said.

"You'll be fine. Just try to get along, Louise," she said. "Eric is Eric."

Before my day began, I was in the washroom checking how I looked. I had a front tooth that was slightly crooked, a pill-bottle nose and hair that looked like black licorice sticks spilling out of a bag. Yea, I know. I know. I dyed my hair again, like everyone does. I traced each of my mirror shapes and exhaled slowly. You see, when I was away from the Daycare Learning Company, I was an artist and often hoped my work would one day be on display in various galleries around town. And I studied just about everyone in the Daycare Learning Company because I needed ideas for my art. Lately, however, I noticed that people didn't spend too much time around me anymore because they felt awkward about ending up in one of my paintings. How did I know this? Last week, someone made me promise not to have her face on a wall, like a wanted poster in a post office. Maybe, it was also because of the way I peered at everyone and then winked with a thumbs-up signal, as if I had just completed a sketch behind my eyes. MB didn't miss much and I'm sure she knew what I was doing.

She was on to me because she suddenly stood directly in front of my desk, hands on hips and her jaw jutting towards me, as if she were daring me to capture her stance in a future painting.

"Go ahead, Louise. Do me."

Sometimes, MB ran the reception area like a strong, but cross-eyed, mother hen. And today it seemed as if she were saving up her dares.

Then, MB mysteriously relaxed right there in front of me. She displayed a gentle but insistent curiosity and asked, "Why don't you do a sketch of me right now, Louise? I would love that!"

"What about that work you want me to do with Eric?" I asked.

"It can wait!" she said

So, I grabbed a sheet of bond paper from the photocopy machine and began my pencil sketch. "Should I just stand here?" MB asked.

"Just be yourself," I said. And right then and there I felt my slightly crooked tooth straightening out and then disappearing under my attentive lips.

The reception area became as still as a warm June day and I was amazed at how quickly I sketched MB's face. Even the phones kept ringing, as if they were celebrating something.

* * *

I just came back to work after having a few days off due to stress and I heard myself saying, "Irene, maybe you're too old to continue being a mother hen in this overpriced daycare."

My nerves were so bad that my insides froze and I became an Inuit woman frozen to the ice of desparation. However, returning to the Daycare Learning Company might be a big mistake.

Halfway through the day, I broke the sound barrier for the first time by yelling at MB for suggesting that I needed more time off work. How dare that sanctimonious blob of a woman hint that I was not fit for employment! Didn't help that I was hung over today too; maybe, I should have called Room Service and had them send up a new head for me. The other Daycare Learning Company people knew me from the past and tiptoed around my eggshells. The look in MB's eyes told me that she wanted me back on long-term disability; she remained silent, then calmly said: "Irene, we'll talk later." I'd love to get that MB bitch fired and she knew it too but I just couldn't get a rise out of her today.

At the end of the day, MB asked to see me in her office. With her were two women, one of whom I recognized from somewhere. "We're from the Renfrew Detox Centre," one of the women said.

"I know why you're here today but I'm not... a drunk," I said.

"I'll leave you three alone," MB said, gently closing her office door, as if its hinges were attached to a fuse.

"We know what to do," the familiar-looking woman said.

"Will someone tell me what that is and why you're doing it?" I begged. "I have rights!"

"Have a seat," the other woman said. "Want a coffee, Irene?" the other woman asked.

"Sure. Why not?"

"Cream?"

"No thanks."

"Sugar?"

"Just black, please."

"Now, Irene, are you having any problems with alcohol?"

"Naw. Not me. I only crave booze when I think of people like MB."

"What you're saying is quite serious, Irene!" the familiar woman said. "And I think your boss has your best interests at heart."

"Right, but can you get MB to go on long-term disability?"

"And how will that help you?" the other woman said. "Why should she be on long-term disability?"

"You have no idea what goes on around here!" I shouted.

"Tell us all about it," the familiar woman said.

"Where do I start?"

"At the beginning," both women said at the same time.

"Mine or hers?"

* * *

I was Louise who came from somewhere else.

Doesn't matter if I'm happy, sad or in-between, my light blue eyes looked like they originated from a planet, maybe of my own making.

And at coffee this morning, I was sitting on the opposite side of the room from MB, boiling in my own resentment because it was all coming back to me and I didn't want MB sticking her mouth in my personal life. Her nose I could deal with by just ignoring it.

Then the somewhere else of my alcoholic father's voice yelled at me and said, "Louise, it's about your natural stupidity… ."

And a half-hour later, my father was funny, charming, warm,

quite drunk, shoving a fifty dollar bill into my right hand and said, "Louise, why don't you treat yourself and go buy some new clothes? You're a natural shopper. A smart woman."

When I grabbed my coffee cup, my knuckles were white pebbles ready to burst from my skin and aimed at my still-alive father. Yea, I was sick. I wanted help but didn't know where to get it. A woman colleague friend next to me suggested a twelve-step program for those who were brought up with boozers in their lives. My fist loosened its grip on the coffee cup and my knuckles became a letter-less keyboard.

Then, I thought of my much older brother who was supposed to be retired but was still working a few nights a week in a dance club until three a.m. He had been sour, grumpy and a dead man walking since his twenties anyway but now he was worse. Yet, he was loyal and had a heart bigger than any coffin; he went out of his way to help a friend with anything – including lending time or money. My brother was a strange mix! Yet, I wanted him to laugh so badly – especially at himself. Laughter was a fifth wheel on his vehicle. My brother was living over his head and his wife told me a year ago that they couldn't afford to live in their own house anymore. Yet, he was taking his wife to Europe – again this summer! His own brother-in-law once laughed and recently told me that my brother had champagne tastes on a draft beer budget but in actual fact, had no taste buds at all – Mister Big Time Operator. And my brother, largely driven by fear, tried to compensate for all the extra weight he carried around by buying designer clothes which made him look like an overstuffed, Tommy clown. I wish I knew what had our booze home done to my brother? And did I ever tell you about his kindness?

"Think I'll invent my own alphabet and compose that letter I've been meaning to write to my father," I said to a colleague friend sitting next to me. "Something about feelings being like fingerprints. You know – unique but not bad."

"Should I know about these feelings and fingerprints?" MB asked suddenly appearing out of nowhere.

"Study my fingers," I said holding my hands up like two claws.

Outside, a mother of a cloud moved closer to the window and I knew, yes I knew, I was Louise and I came from somewhere else.

* * *

There I was with all my years of experience and MB needed me again to review a problem file involving a possible lawsuit from a parent. She only called me when she required my expertise, which was good. You know consultants are sometimes seen as people who borrow your shoes to show you how to walk. Today, however, I was really needed.

As soon as I arrived at the Daycare Learning Company, MB handed me the folder and I went into the staffroom where I plunked myself down at a table. I was alone. Not three minutes into my reading, MB appeared and slid into a chair beside me.

"I took one of my sons to the Calgary Flames game last night," she said. "Sometimes, he jumped up and cheered or yelled at the players or officials and I had to tell him to sit down numerous times because that wasn't how anyone should behave in public. That kid needed, really needed more impulse control or self-restraint. You know about that emotional intelligence, don't you? Embarrassing was what my son was! He blamed everybody, including the popcorn vendor when the Flames fell behind by one goal. He allowed negative feelings to dominate. My boy acted without reasoning or logic when the replay on the electronic scoreboard showed that a player was offside after a goal was disallowed. He carried grudges; was unforgiving of the referee. That son of mine wasn't a good listener when I tried to explain a penalty shot by the visiting team. He acted out when there was a problem, like when the Flames had to play with one man in the penalty box."

"You want to talk about your son instead of this file?" I asked.

"Only for a minute or two, Jim. I know you have work to do and so do I," she said.

"Have to use the washroom. Be back in a second," I said.

In the bathroom mirror, I saw a calm, methodical, sagging face that was receptive to the pain of others. After, I washed my hands and dried them with paper towel. Then, I rolled the damp paper towel into a ball and tossed it away.

"He shoots, he scores!" I said to myself. Then I looked more closely in the mirror and took a deep breath. Time I got back to MB.

"You know what? I was at that game last night too," I told her.

"No kidding, Jim! Where were you sitting?"

"Way up in the cheap seats. But you know – I loved the smell of the damp ice, even from up there. And I got a kick out of the way the fans or players teased each other during the warm-up – like boys in men suits. I also enjoyed the thumping body checks, the officials calling a penalty behind the play, the deking, the crisp passing and the finesse. I even liked the sounds of sticks or the puck hitting the boards or that clanging sound when the puck hits a goalpost. And sometimes fighting removed the tension from a game. My favorite was seeing a player come in on a breakaway and watching the moves. Beautiful stuff! Like poetry."

"But what does poetry have to do with my son getting too excited?"

"Didn't you see the way Makarov changed speeds and made those incredible moves of his. He even faked out an entire section of fans. Rows of them shifted in their seats. Beautiful! Poetry, I tell you. Poetry!"

"I'll let you get back to your file, Jim," MB said.

There I was with all my years of experience and MB needed me again.

* * *

Uppermost in my mind was that I liked to look good and dress fine. And when I walked into MB's office on this February morning, my tan was deep and my teeth felt like rows of perfectly, white headstones. My blue jeans were pressed and could be creased blue cardboard sheets folded around my legs but that's how I liked them. My brown tweed sports jacket was made for my shoulders. My shirt was shocking pink in colour and my necktie was a dark, blue knitted masterpiece. When I offered advice to MB about testing a student, she said, "Jim, you do things so calmly around here that you should consider working as a late-night, FM radio announcer some day. Or you could be one of those coolheaded, well-dressed, TV newscasters."

And I couldn't help but flash my Hollywood smile at her.

"Thank you. Maybe, I missed my calling," I said.

"Can I buy you lunch today, Jim?"

"Thanks, but I can't do it today. Have to get to another Daycare Learning Company branch before one o'clock."

"I understand," she said. "How about next week?"

"I'll have to check my schedule."

"Let me know."

I wasn't used to the boss being so friendly and I'd rather just have a mineral water for lunch anyway, so I didn't stain my teeth or lighten my tan. Because they were still baking from yesterday's tanning salon, my lips said little.

"Don't you ever worry about skin cancer?" she asked as she got closer and almost touched my neck with an index finger.

"Naw, it's not like lying on a beach. Besides, we're all going to die sometime," I said taking a step back from her. "I want to be looking good when I join that final parade."

"Even your lips look tanned," she said.

"They are. I don't have a spot on my body that hasn't been kissed by the sun," I said licking my lips back to life."

"Yea, the kiss of death," she said.

"Right. Oh… I just remembered that I'm quite busy for the next week or so. I'll have to get back to you about lunch."

"Did I say something to offend you, Jim? It's just that there's been so much talk about melanoma lately and I…"

"I know you mean well but look carefully," I said, pointing to my mouth. "My lips have lives of their own."

* * *

I wished people would stop staring at my thirty-eight D boobs. Even MB, who was fairly well-endowed herself, often gave my chest a second look because my breasts were enormous. To keep eyes off my boobs today, I wore my chestnut brown wig long and let the strands hang over my chest. The rest of me was nice too, although I heard Eric say that even though I loved dogs and rabbits, I had a bitchy, irritating voice, the face of a horse with a double-chin, an oversized misshaped nose and the mental agility of a doorknob. Boy, I showed him what this horse-face could do to an idiot like him! Yea, his voice got higher for several seconds when I finished him off alone in his office. Let me tell you! I was Angie. I was a smart woman, you know. I lived on my own and did my own home repairs – like last month when I installed hardwood floors all on my own. Angie, The Sexy Reno Queen, was what I called myself.

Aside from working here at the Daycare Learning Company, I was also an artist. I painted and I made clay pots. Besides being very creative, I loved music, especially women folk singers and a group called Blue Rodeo. Actually, I enjoyed all kinds of music, even old rock music from the sixties and seventies, like Led Zeppelin. I liked to wear black clothes although a girlfriend once told me that black was too dark for my fair complexion.

"Makes your skin look chalky, Angie!" she said.

Didn't matter what she said. I loved black!

I also liked dressing up in my Victoria Secret underwear because I looked so good in them. Usually when I felt that way,

I brought home a man, only if he promised me lots of stamina all night. Sleeping I could do anytime.

Men who approached me professionally in the Daycare Learning Company had only one thing in mind and one thing only and it wasn't students. I could tell. They usually tried extra carefully to carry on a conversation that revolved around work or music or art. After a short while, they tried too hard to not watch my nipples. At that point, I made some excuse to leave the room, sometimes forcefully. Occasionally, a man would follow me out of the room and down the hallway like a puppy dog. Funny thing about men: if you showed them just a little attention, they rolled over on their backs and you could do anything with them.

I considered breast reduction surgery but I heard it was painful. Instead, I pretended like crazy.

* * *

Right! It was me, Michael, the squeaky clean jock and I was getting married. Some people said that I was a well-oiled man machine! My father, who was a Missionary Boss in Nova Scotia, would be proud. I was going into administration too. A colleague told me yesterday that I'd make a great administrator because I have that stern, pained look on my face, as if I were born with hemorrhoids or constipation or both. I just laughed and ignored him. And just last week, I overheard our MB whispering loudly to Eric, "That Michael would be better suited for collecting bottles and cans."

Nice. Everyone around here was so, so supportive. Also, some of the other women gave me a hard time about looking like an oversized Boy Scout. What a bunch of clichés! They'll see. I'll show 'em.

At lunch today, I was told that some of the male staff members were planning a bachelor party for me.

"We're coming too," two women said.

"It's for guys only," a man at my table said.

"I want to be invited too," said MB, suddenly appearing in the staffroom.

"Sorry, you can't. It's for men only!"

"Are you telling us that we can't come because we're woman?" MB snarled.

"Exactly,' I said. "I'm the one getting married and this stag party is only for guys! You didn't hear us demanding to go to your showers did you? That's the way it is. And leave that gender politics game in a hole somewhere, will ya!"

"You think so, eh?"

"We know so," two men laughed.

"You two wouldn't even know the link between sex and pregnancy," another woman said.

"Unless you want to pop out of a cake," I said. "Keep your skirts on, will ya!"

"Go sell your Boy Scout cookies, Michael!" a third woman said. "You remind me of the guy who stole a clock and didn't realize that he was facing time!"

"And you think you might have a hand in all that?" the man beside me said.

"Okay. Okay. This is getting ridiculous, Michael. That's enough everyone!" MB shouted. "That conduct is not very professional. Each of you, straighten up right now!"

"Should I get back to my profession – you know, collecting

bottles and cans?" I asked MB, trying to cut the room tension, which was as hard as a stale oatmeal cookie.

"Give it a rest, Michael" she said. "Have fun and then just go get married, please!"

Just as an enormous smile crept across MB's face, I thought about inviting her and only her to my bachelor party.

* * *

A close friend on staff said this morning, "Irene, know something? You carry that headache of yours around like some kind of cross."

Every time the migraine pain starts, I brush my silver hair harder and harder back behind my ears hoping to wipe the throbbing from my head. Sometimes, I look in the mirror and watch my dark eyes pound in unison with the pain. Then, the same eyes almost split in half from the aching. Migraines – they crippled me! And I am letting myself go too. If I gain five to ten more pounds, I look noticeably overweight. Also, I don't dress as snazzy as I used to and I care less and less about my make-up. But I suit up and show up for work. Even MB surprised me yesterday with her compassion when she said, "Irene, I know you are not far off from retirement and I respect you for just showing up at work every day with that awful aching head of yours!".

At lunch today, the pain was so, so bad that my face felt like it was folding back on itself. I told MB that I would be going home to bed immediately after work and would miss the staff meeting.

"Of course, go ahead, Irene," she said.

I think we've all been too hard on MB.

Anyhow, I've tried doctor after doctor, pill after pill. Nothing works. Meditation helps a little bit; I'm a firm believer in spirituality in any form, so praying helps too.

Later, while watching MB with her look of sympathy from across the staffroom, I could tell that she understood my desperation and I appreciated her distanced concern.

When I got home, I ate a quick, light supper. Then, I laid my silver head on my huge, puffy pillow where I tried to wipe away my frown, like sweat. I unplugged the phone and told my husband not to disturb me for any reason. Gradually I allowed my determination to will away the throbbing and it eventually left me, as it fell to the floor, like a heavy winter boot. After, I concentrated on my own notion of a power bigger than I was and offered thanks for the suffering. At the same time, I meditated so I could find out what I was supposed to learn from all this torment and ask to have the aching rinsed away. Apparently, this spiritual force was a gentleman or gentlewoman and would not intervene unless asked. And I prayed for sleep with quiet persistence.

Finally, in my sleep, the pounding vanished and I wore the world like a loose-fitting robe.

* * *

Whenever I came to the Daycare Learning Company for my consultant job, I felt like that sleeping boy emerging from a grandmother quilt; I knew I had to feel rested for this place.

As soon as I walk in the front door, my breathing becomes that exhaling pattern of a psychologist and, while nodding my head, I rub my eyes before paying careful attention to what is being asked of me. People say I am a great listener and I play the part well. This morning, staff hit me with a barrage of questions. Even MB had her own written list of requests:

"Jim, what do these non-verbal testing scores mean? How quickly can I get a speech pathologist in here? I have a student who should be screened for Attention Deficit Disorder." Michael wanted me to immediately confirm the need for an intellectual assessment. "Jim, I need to find out more about this kid in my class!"

All of this before I could read the student's file or even spoon coffee whitener into my cup. And Angie wanted me to visit her classroom to observe a student's defiant behaviour.

"This boy is driving me nuts, Jim!" she said. "I don't know if he can't or won't behave!"

Both wanted answers right now. First, I got up from my chair, poured myself a cup of coffee and stirred until the whitener disappeared in my cup. Next, I stood at the counter and savored my coffee before tasting their requests. Then, I acknowledged each Daycare Learning Company concern with a nod and said to Michael and Angie in a voice as calm as smoke, "Please hold on for a moment, will you, so I can drink my second mouthful of coffee."

One after another, they droned on and on about their plights, like two-legged anxiety machines. And they were all good people too. That was my cue. Wrapping myself in the textures and smells of my grandmother's quilt – the multicoloured patches of every material imaginable – I was momentarily protected from this blizzard of Daycare Learning Company words. Those soft, grandmother patterns did it for me every time. Thinking of my grandma now made far more sense while listening to Michael and Angie.

Most acquaintances, friends and family thought there was no order to the design of my grandma's relationship but I knew better. Nobody ever gave my grandma and her new boyfriend any suggestions about the novelty of their relationship; the same boyfriend who had a wooden leg until she broke it off. And nobody asked so many questions, like Michael and Angie did.

"Jim, you look a little out of it today. Did you hear what I said?" Michael asked.

"Are you with us today, Jim?" asked Angie.

"Sure. Of course. I haven't missed a word. My grandmother taught me how to listen."

Yes, she would be proud.

And I suppose that life without the unique geometry of this place would be pointless anyway.

* * *

I needed to talk to MB about my role around here. After all, I was her Assistant Principal. Budget and scheduling were but two of my duties but she also expected me to keep my finger on the pulse of the staff. MB wanted me to do this by trying to blend in with the staff so I could let her know if there was anything going on behind her back.

Yes, it looked like I enjoyed sticking my nose into personal business by being friendly with everyone because it was one of my administrative duties. The boss taught me well and appreciated my efforts, especially when there was an obvious conflict between staff members or with MB herself.

However, I had difficulty "blending" with Louise though. Last week, she got angry with me while I was pretending to search for a file in the office. She said, "Know something, Eric? There are people around here who really trust you to keep your word but you have no identity of your own, which is why you have your nose buried up MB's butt so often."

"Thanks, Louise. Still trying to win friends and influence people eh, Louise?" I asked. "Are you trying to get fired or something?"

"You don't scare me, Eric. I've been here much longer than you have and I'll still be here when you're gone!"

"That's right, Louise. You've been here since Napoleon was a cadet."

"Longer."

What did Louise know anyway? She wasn't even a member of administration. And wait till I tell MB what Louise said to me!

Yet, Louise's words aroused me. For some strange reason, I suddenly believed I was the most trustworthy and sexiest man alive, even though I carried several more pounds than my skeleton could bear. I always felt sexier after being hurt.

Today, I wore a light blue shirt, which hung out from my white polyester slacks. My hair curled at my neck and rust-coloured eyeglasses gave me a look that could go from stern to glad in two seconds. It was just my way of protecting my duties around here. Someone had to do it! However, I wished other staff members hadn't sat at least two chairs away from me at lunchtime. After all, I could be the most trustworthy and sexiest man in the Daycare Learning Company whenever I wanted to and I was not responsible for my own behaviour. If only more staff knew about these sides of me!

Oh, there's the boss and I should find out why she was laughing so hard! I had an expressive personality type so she understood why I wanted to share the laugh. I'll go ask her. What? She walked away from me. Do I smell bad or something?

"Gotta make an important phone call, Eric," she said to me over her shoulder.

"But I need to talk to you about something."

"Is it personal?"

"It's about me being more effective around here."

"Oh, that can wait until later!"

"But. . . ."

"Later!"

"What's so funny about that earlier joke?" I asked, hoping that would make her spend some time with me.

"Later," she said. "Didn't you hear me the first time, Eric?"

Right then, I tried to walk in her shoes and I could tell there would be no "later" today.

* * *

I worry a lot when I am not being the boss.

This morning, when I went to get my newspaper, I heard a perfect "wolf whistle". Thinking that the whistle was directed at me, I pulled up the shoulder strap of my nightgown and scampered back into the house. Who the hell was whistling at me? Then, I peeked between my living-room curtains and checked outside. Nobody was there. Next, I ran to the kitchen and looked out my back door. I surveyed the yard but nobody was there. It was then that I realized that the "wolf whistle" may have originated from inside my house but from whom and where? Then, I was really worried!

I trotted into my bedroom and quickly got dressed. Maybe, just maybe, my husband was playing a trick on me. That bugger must be hiding somewhere! Yet, I'm sure I saw him leave for work about ten minutes ago.

I walked into the living room and studied our cockatoo, a big, red-crested bird, perched in its cage and hanging from the living room ceiling. No, it couldn't be! That bird only sang songs and then quite rigidly stopped in the middle of each piece, throwing in a few bars from totally unrelated songs such as *O Canada*, *Louie Louie*, *The Camptown Races* or *House of The Rising Sun*. However, a "wolf whistle" has never been heard from its cage.

When I arrived at the Daycare Learning Company, still worrying aloud about the source of the "wolf whistle", Eric made me feel like a kid making excuses to an adult.

"Did your cockatoo maintain eye contact with you at all times? All members of the male species do the same thing when they 'wolf whistle'. Males don't hide their admiration."

"Sure, Eric," I said. "And you represent the male species, do you?"

"Last time I looked in the mirror, it looked that way."

"Got any other advice for me?"

"Later."

"Good!"

"Do you know how to 'wolf whistle', Eric?"

"Nope."

"Are you sure?"

"Absolutely!"

"Absolutely what, Eric?"

"Absolutely not!"

"Didn't think you had it in you."

"What?"

"A wolf whistle."

"Gee, thanks."

"And do you still need to have that talk with me, Eric?" I asked.

"Later," he said. "Later."

Then, I moved towards my office before Eric could say another word and watched the phone buttons light up under the sirens of my freshly polished fingernails.

"Tell Louise to hold all my calls, Eric. I need to find out something." I said closing my office door.

* * *

When I looked into the washroom mirror, I couldn't believe what I saw. There I was in plain view. Me, Angie, with tar-coloured hair (this time) with both eyes and a mouth that protruded as if I'd spent years teaching newly arrived immigrants how to pronounce the word "open". My image amazed me.

"I love your big, shiny eyes, Angie," my current boyfriend said to me the other day. "They're as big as stopwatches. They're beauties! And your mouth, I could eat!"

"Thanks," I said. "Now, here's something for you. Open... wide!"

Even though my eyes protruded a bit too much because I had a thyroid condition called exophthalmia, I thought they were strong eyes. But they didn't get that way overnight. Maybe, it was the memories that amazed me today.

I've had to be tough because my ex-husband once took off with our daughter, our only child, when we lived in Parry Sound, Ontario. After I found them both in a Montreal motel, I was given full custody and my ex was thrown in jail. I couldn't let my daughter out of my sight after that! Later, we secretly moved to Calgary in case my ex escaped from jail or was given one of those early, bleeding heart paroles. Yea, it was a long story and couldn't be told in front of a mirror. Besides, MB wanted to use the washroom. I had better get going! My privacy was my only protection.

Just a couple of weeks ago, I returned from a holiday on a Caribbean island. My current man couldn't get away from his work so I went with a girlfriend instead. My friend and I were constantly scrutinized by several black men, women and children, maybe because whites were rarely seen in this part of town. At the time, we were both too astounded by the staring to be scared. Soon, a tiny black man approached us and said, "Da only whites with such enchanting big eyes I ever seen are whites on wheels or whites in closed cars or tour buses. Were you born with dose magnificent eyes? Bet your lover, he crazy about dem eyes, eh? And dat mouth, it want to eat da world too eh."

When I came down the hallway of the Daycare Learning Company, I tossed aside my privacy and shook with laughter as I told everyone and anyone that I was "the first white Angie not on wheels" and that my daughter was still safe and doing just fine. Some staff members were puzzled. Most laughed along with me after I explained the story of my eyes and mouth.

Before long, laughter tears poured down my white-red cheeks. My "O" mouth was a half-moon mouth. And even the beliefs behind my laughing didn't make me feel bad because I was white.

Today, I knew for the first time what was meant by the word "open" and gawd, it felt so good!

* * *

Today, I was dressed in my killer Angie outfit, a purple and red mini-skirt and black blouse. My hair was tied in a rope-like ponytail and my mind told me my face was a painting this morning. I also took an assortment of vitamin pills every morning because my insides needed to feel as good as my outsides.

I was the oldest of a family of eight kids and once thought that I was in no hurry to have kids of my own. Working with kids all day didn't make me anxious to go home to them. But, like my hair colour, I changed. And I had a daughter of my own.

Someone on staff said the other day, "Angie, you have a strong elegance and an independence that would flatter any woman, any mother."

"Well, thank you for your kind words. Would you mind letting MB and Eric know that too?" I said.

"Sure thing," they replied.

Yesterday, I walked by MB near the main office and thought of sharing those good words from staff members with her but changed my mind when she opened her mouth wide enough just to breathe. I kept going past her down the hallway because I wasn't sure what was coming after the breathing.

"You look like a vitamin beauty today, Angie," a male colleague said to me in the hallway. "Do your insides look as good as your outsides?"

"Yes and thank you. I feel great!" I said stopping right there in my high heels, almost carving my initials into the floor. "Tell that to MB and Eric, will ya."

"Good idea," he said.

Then, my eyes swept the hallway floor, not because I was embarrassed but because that was my way of thinking before speaking and I could feel a joke coming towards me.

After, the same colleague looked around and, seeing that no one else was around, asked, "Did you hear the one about the man who had to undergo a second circumcision? Well the same guy also had no eyelids. So the doctor said he'd fix both. When the man came home to his wife, he asked how he looked and she replied 'cockeyed'."

"That joke was very hard on me."

"Then you'd better keep a stiff upper lid," he said.

"Remind me to keep both eyes opened whenever I pass you in the hallway again."

"Or, you could simply cut around me."

"Do you always operate like that?"

"Only when I zip around you. By the way, have you ever thought of having yourself bottled, like those vitamins you take?"

"Flattery will get you everywhere!"

"And where would that be?" he asked.

How did he know? How did he know that I liked men who were witty, who had more gray matter than a tube of putty and who never took themselves too seriously. They killed me. They really did! And in my sexy outfit, I stayed ahead of the game.

* * *

"You look trim, Michael. Your daily jogging has paid off," Angie said as I ambled through the staffroom.

"Thanks, Angie" I said. "I feel good too."

If anyone was ever enthusiastic about sweat recently, it was me. When I felt this child-like happiness, it was because I was sweating like other people cried.

However, a few days ago, I told off MB because she was treating me like a kid after I came in from a great lunchtime jogging session. That woman was always on a mission to have the right answer. Perhaps, it was because her ego told her she had to be right, never happy. All I did was offer a solution to the over-usage of the photocopy machines at a staff meeting. What was the big deal?

"Why not get each Daycare Learning Company employee to punch in a personal number code every time he or she used a machine?" I offered.

Colleagues seemed confused when MB said, "Michael, you must be a child if you think everything needs to be counted around here, like candy or toys!"

"Then, what do you suggest?" I asked.

"I think we all should behave maturely and use the honour system."

"Right," I said. "Mature. Honour system."

Now, after re-playing what happened with MB, I was resting in a corner of the lunchroom after my noon-hour run.

"You know, I come from a family of twelve. There was standing room only in the playpen and I fought for the least amount of attention from anyone. Even today I still cling to the leftovers of my mother's tenderness after my brothers and sisters have had their full. That was our family hieroglyphics. Maybe that's why I hated being treated like a child and felt comfortable punching in codes. It all reminded me of leftovers," I told Angie.

"There's nothing wrong with codes, Michael. Hey, look outside! We might be in for some showers," Angie said.

"Yea, they're predicting a downpour."

Then, rain the size of miniature mirrors began splattering on the staffroom window. Most of the staff came prepared with a raincoat, an umbrella or both. I was the only one who had to scamper out to the parking lot with an empty box, that once contained packages of photocopying paper, to shield my head and shoulders. But I was also the one wearing a peaceful smile under a soggy cardboard flap. There was something tender about that rain when I was outside running – even to my car and my feet sounded like that constant clicking of a photocopy machine.

"What happened to all those pounds, Michael!" Angie shouted as I unlocked my car door. "You look good, really good!"

* * *

Here I was minding my own business by the staffroom sink spooning strawberry yogurt behind my teeth. Sometimes, when MB stared at me, I felt as if she were saying, "Michael, you're committing a sacrilege against health foods!" In my head I asked, "What do you mean?"

And then a committee of idiots would continue the dialogue.

"You and yogurt just don't go together."

"How do you know that?"

"I know you like to jog every day, Michael but aren't you more of a beer and pretzels kind of guy?"

"You drink Diet Coke and eat chocolate bars. What does that make you?"

"How does this have any bearing on you eating strawberry yogurt?"

"Right," I said.

"Thought you didn't understand my question, Michael," MB said after clearing her throat.

And I worked so hard at smelling like a rose around here. Yes, I did such a good job. The best!

The boss looked like she was ready to sneak up behind me and pinch one of my petals to find out if I was a real rose or not. The nerve of MB! Sure, I'll give her something to pinch! I looked like I smelled. Or, I smelled like I looked – a rose. That's it! Nothing complicated. Maybe, when I get home tonight I'll ask my boy-scout leader, lawyer wife what to do about her.

Oh. Oh. MB's coming back towards me.

'Tell me something, Michael, were you born in Canada?" she asked.

I nearly choked on my yogurt and flashed my spoon at her, like a tentative knife.

"Of course, I was born in Nova Scotia and then moved to Lethbridge when I was a kid. Why do you ask?"

I wanted her to say something about my coffee-coloured skin, my dark features but MB said,

"Easy does it! Thought you might have some Hindu

blood in you. Most of us do come from somewhere else, you know."

"I agree but what makes you think I have some Hindu blood in me?"

"Take a guess," MB replied.

"You should get a job with the United Nations," I said, trying very hard to restrain myself from laughing aloud.

Then, she moved a few feet away from me, her eyes looking like they wanted to explode from her head. Laughter eyes. Maybe, she wanted me to consider a skin transplant so I could look cleaner, whiter, because roses with lighter hues smelled sweeter, I think. Or perhaps, she wanted to drop one of her sanctimonious aphrodisiacs into my strawberry yogurt when I wasn't looking. I watched. I watched her carefully.

* * *

I puffed up my thick, fire-red hair which I just dyed again a couple of weeks ago and finger-counted the brown beads on the freckle necklace around my neck. A couple of us women really liked dying our hair. My skin now looked so pale. I felt like a shy woman trapped inside a gregarious skin and believe me I was not known to be bashful. Yet, whenever I heard someone tell a sex joke, an involuntary blood ocean worked its way through my pale-white skin from my toes to my forehead. Before I knew it, I was floating on my own red sea. Yet, I knew. I knew over the years that women told far better dirty jokes than men do.

"Maybe, it's the change in my hair colour that makes it worse," I told myself. "That shiny red colour. All I know is that

I can't get it to stop and people insist on telling me jokes just so they can see my skin turn red. And it seems I get redder if the joke is told in a low voice."

"Hey, Louise – did you hear the one about the hooker who had the initials T.L.C. tattooed on her lower belly?" Angie whispered into my ear just outside the washroom door.

"Do the initials mean Tender Loving Care, Angie?" I whispered back.

"No, Tight Little Coochie."

"Must be an old tattoo," I told her.

Even with my quick comeback, it happened again.

MB walked into the staffroom immediately after the joke had been told. She wondered aloud about all the laughter and saw me armchair-slumped in a red puddle.

"Something wrong, Louise?" she asked.

"No," I answered, my eyes swelling with tears.

"Come on, what's the matter, Louise?"

"Relax, MB! I can handle it," I said.

Moments later, my uncontrollable skin felt better. Yet, I wished I could do something about how I felt. It wasn't the sex that did it. I could tell those raunchy jokes with the best of them! It's just that my uncle was a big shot downtown at head office. He'd want me to be stronger and probably hoped I would ignore anything that made my skin turn red. And I was even more embarrassed that everyone knew my uncle was a big shot downtown.

When the staffroom quieted down, I proclaimed to everyone around me that I'd be spending my Christmas vacation in my uncle's Hawaiian condo to give my freckles a chance to get together.

"That's funny," Angie announced. "So you're going on a holiday to join the dots and make yourself whole again. Just like that hooker, eh?"

* * *

I slid smoothly into my chair and settled myself. Across from me, the Zone Superintendent looked like a silent gunfighter who rehearsed his laughter before a kill and rarely lost a fight. With the tall, wiry frame of a jogger, the Big Boss from Central Office flashed his sky blue eyes at me and tilted a gray-fringed bald head to one side. Rumor had it that he hated exercise and chain-smoked cigarettes in his car while driving from one Daycare Learning Company branch to another. I could smell the smoke on his clothes. He looked too naïve to be political and I bet he was not part of the inner circle in downtown administration.

"So, Eric, do you plan on being an Assistant Principal for the rest of your career?" he suddenly asked me. "Or, do you want to run your own school one day?"

"Not sure yet. Think I need more time to make a decision."

"No pressure, Eric."

Little did he know that I tried administration strictly out of curiosity and for no other reason. And I was planning to leave. Why? The forces in my head were largely nurtured by imagination, open-mindedness, intuition, daring and were becoming hostile to the restrictions of administration. The administrative minds around me were all starved of imagination, narrow, rational, circumspect and obsessed with control and conformity. Maybe, creativity and administration were like the prudish husband and the roistering wife who were either throwing dishes at each other or sulking in silence.

"When will you make a decision? And…can I help in any way?" he asked.

"You already have," I said.

"Excellent!" he said. "Just what I want to hear. Want to talk about it?"

"Maybe another time. Like I said, I want to reflect on this some more."

"Are you sure, Eric?"

"As sure as I'm sitting here," I said.

"Okay," he said almost leaping to his feet. "I have to go!"

"Me too. There's something I need to do."

* * *

Today, my long shiny hair was the colour of rust and I felt like living and breathing anything from Ireland even though I wasn't Irish. Must have been that TV, soap commercial I kept seeing recently. There was a lilt in my voice and a song in my brain. However, beneath all that, was a temper that could strip the bark off a maple tree.

Right now, Michael was reading MY magazine in the staff-room. How dare he do that! With my hands on my hips, I glared my soap bar Irish eyes at him but he didn't move. Then, I tapped him on the shoulder and motioned with my head to get another magazine. Again, Michael looked up at me, yawned and then resumed his reading.

"Cement underwear may be fine in Ireland, Louise, but in Canada, they eventually shatter," Michael suddenly said turning his head towards me. "You've been watching that TV commercial too much!"

"Is that supposed to be funny, Michael?" I asked.

"Why don't you grab another magazine, Louise? There are lots over there."

"I don't want those OVER THERE."

"What is your problem?"

"You!" I snarled.

"I hear something crumbling, Louise. Be careful how you sit down," Michael said.

Then, I moved away to another seat and swore that vengeance was forthcoming, moments from now.

After strutting back into the main office area, I waited by the counter for my turn at the photocopy machine. A song that only I could hear caused me to shake my hips and shuffle my feet as I planned what I was going to do with Michael, the chair thief.

The boss walked by and said, "Louise, you look so sharp, so young but poised today. You know – mature."

"Thanks, MB," I replied in a low enough voice that she didn't hear me.

And right away, my skin crawled back on itself. MB had probably skipped childhood because her barometer insisted that everyone around her must behave like overripe prunes. Maturity was her favorite dogma.

Meanwhile, I drifted off to the sounds of the humming photocopy machine. Yet, I'd rather be on the roof sorting airmail than singing the mature songs of MB. And, as I saw myself on the roof, I had my revenge by seeing Crazy Glue being carefully squeezed on Michael's zipper. His pants were so tight that they had their own alphabet and I… I was living and breathing everything Irish again.

* * *

I saved lives.

Here I was in MB's office on what was probably the hardest chair in the room, one of those high, straight back, wooden ones. I felt my lined forehead tighten even more as I prepared myself for the saving of the boss's life. I noticed she was more and more worried about staff members wanting to get rid of her so I pretended that she was still in charge of this moment but really contemplated important issues, like the shirts I needed to buy after work and my family.

Today, I wore tan-coloured slacks and a bright yellow sweater so I appeared easy-going for my purpose. I thought of my five-year old daughter who was allergic to so many different items including: peanut butter, dust, cats, dairy products to name but a few; my daughter needed some kind of saving just about every day. Thank goodness, my wife never seemed to need any help because of her high-paying accountant job with an oil company and she provided me with that feeling that all of us would live forever. This was especially true when I occasionally went on a business trip with her and the last thought on my mind was throwing someone a life preserver.

"The entire staff hates me, Eric," MB finally said.

"Why do you say that?" I asked titling my head to one side.

"Look at how they behave when I walk into the staffroom.

I've tried to be nice. I've tried to feel like they feel. What's that called again, Eric?"

"Empathy," I said.

"Yea, I've tried that empathy stuff but nothing works! They don't trust me."

"I trust you," I said.

"Yea, but you're my Assistant Principal. You're in that middle place between administration and staff. I know you've had some run-in's with staff but I'll bet most of the Daycare Learning Company people trust you more than they trust me – including the Caretaker, the Secretaries, the Aides, the Librarian and on and on."

"You're starting to sound like one of those Viagra stories," I say. "You know – being too rigid."

"Is that supposed to make me feel better, Eric?"

"Get a grip on it, will ya!"

"Trying to be funny again, Eric?"

" No, not at all. That's something you'd say to me."

"Do I sound like that?"

"Hey, I'm the Assistant Boss Man. I'm here to save you! Remember? It's my turn."

"Bet you hadn't planned on me floundering like this?"

No, I hadn't expected to see MB being so vulnerable.

"But you'll have to save yourself," I said. "Isn't that what you're always trying to do with everyone around here anyway? Follow your own advice – whatever that is."

"Don't forget, what we shared today stays within these four walls. Right?"

"Exactly what have we shared?"

"Me being caught with my emotional drawers down."

"Of course, you… your emotional drawers… down. I'm here to save lives." I said crossing my right leg over my left knee. "Like you, right?"

* * *

My lawyer wife, who I sometimes call my girlfriend, was the opposite of any Barbie Doll; she had nothing blonde about her. Ironically, MB said to me the other day, "Michael, sometimes you behave like a grown up toy doll."

"What do you mean?" I asked.

"Well, Michael, you always dress so well, even casually. You look squeaky clean at all hours of the work day. Most times, you're harmless! And I'll bet people play with you too. Bet they could bend your arms and legs any which way."

"That's changing," I said. "And I'd be lost without your intuitive genius."

Initially I was hurt by her comments. But then I agreed with her. However, within the last year or so, I think I learned how to shed the toy doll image after reading several outstanding novels about real life issues, novels that were not on bestseller lists. Too many books to list. And I strongly believed that getting along with other Daycare Learning Company employees was the best quality I had – even though I was mostly a loner and rarely joined staff group conversations. Novel reading told me that my behaviour was acceptable. One on one with staff members, I did a great job. So what if I was pliable sometimes! So what if I was a toy doll!

This morning I walked briskly into MB's office and closed the door. Sometimes, I despised the boss for her toy doll comments but right now, I forgot about all that and trusted her. I had to. After all, MB was the boss and she wasn't all bad. Almost immediately, I became choked up. Tears welled up in my eyes and threatened to spill down my cheeks. I needed to reach out to MB.

"My girlfriend, no my wife, had to be hospitalized last night because of her bad back and the doctors think it's much more than just a bad back," I said to MB.

"Oh, that's awful," she said while giving me a measured, light hug.

"You're a beauty," I murmured. "Read any good novels lately?"

And MB was suddenly lost for words.

"No, I haven't," she finally told me. "But… what are the doctors saying about your wife's – girlfriend's back and what does novel reading have to do with all of this? Oh, and one other question: why do you go back and forth calling her your girlfriend and then your wife?"

"Because she's my babe, I'm her babe and we both couldn't care less about politically correct labels! I'm not sure if that makes any sense. And some novels are about real life pain. I'll find out later today about my girlfriend's back. They saw something on one of her lungs. She used to be a heavy smoker but quit a few months ago. The doctor ordered more X-rays. Thanks for your understanding. People around here don't really know this side of you."

"I appreciate that, Michael."

"Maybe… maybe, there are three sides to you: Side A, Side B. and some kind of truth in the middle."

"I hope so. And good insight on your part, Michael! I apologize for saying you're like a grown up toy doll the other day. And maybe I should read one of those novels."

"That's very classy of you. Thank you! I better clean myself up a bit."

"You look fine, Michael."

"So do you," I said. "So do you."

* * *

I didn't like the odds.

Chances were that everyone was now calling me a Big Time Operator behind my back. I preferred being called MB. What I hated most though was when several staff members stopped talking now whenever I walked into the staffroom. I wondered if it was because I had a point to prove every time I said something. And why were all those fists hidden under the tables? Was I that bad? I was supposed to be in charge around here!

Within the last couple of weeks, I walked with a noticeable limp – the result of a car accident last month. Recently staff members were mocking my gait at every opportunity without any mercy. They thought I didn't notice them doing that behind my sloping back. Everyone knew I once had polio too so my limping was more exaggerated than usual. Before the accident however, the limp was hardly noticeable.

The hell with everyone! I had one of the most expensive houses in the best part of town and owned great season's tickets to the Calgary Flames. Because my brother worked for an airline and was entitled to free passes, I took exotic vacations. I got the best deals on anything from cars to linen. In fact, last weekend I flew to Lisbon for two days and bought this hand-made tablecloth that could be the talk of any staff member's dining-room table.

But I was still hearing second-hand jokes about my green polyester jacket like "What's green, gimpy and waddles all over? The MB Giant."

Mean stuff. Boy, did they ever want me out of here! It reached a point where Louise treated me like a fat piece of lint on her old red dress the other day.

"You're in my way!" she said. "I have lots of work to do!"

And I knew I had a belly. But I didn't like the whispering I heard last week that I was five months pregnant when I had my tubes tied quite a few years ago. Nice.

I also overheard that my husband should keep me on a leash because I probably carried his testicles around in a glass jar of formaldehyde all day in my purse. Very nice indeed.

People who came from Montreal and Toronto said my excuse was that maybe I was born in a place like Antigonish, Nova Scotia (but it was really small town Alberta) where some small shots became big shots often told themselves they could have gone to medical school.

I didn't like the odds.

* * *

The nuns taught me everything I knew.

I was content because I saw the world as being flat. Having one of everything made me very happy. One husband, one set of two sons, one bungalow, one annual holiday spent on my parents' farm – I was a woman of one's for the most part. The only minor conflict was with my husband in that he had a passion for country music and I hated that predictable, one-way, nasal whining. How many times can someone reflect on a sunset or get drunk because of a cheating heart?

My husband told me last week that I should stop kidding myself.

"Know something? You really are a bit of a cowboy yourself. You often think you see everything more clearly than anyone else and maybe that's why they call you those nicknames at work," he said.

Ah, that MB image of mine! Some staff probably thought I had the mental agility of a candlestick. Little did they realize that those nuns were constantly on a humility teaching mission so I wanted to show everyone that I was wise but teachable.

Inside the Daycare Learning Company, I started carrying a very modern briefcase everywhere I went. It was filled with imported chocolate bars to help me on my own mission. These, I occasionally used to bribe any staff member who disagreed with my viewpoints. Sometimes, colleagues refused my precious chocolate and I didn't understand why. they couldn't see horizons as clearly as I did. Like the other day when a staff member told me it was dangerous to live in a cut and dry world after I told her that an answer is either right or wrong most times.

This morning I was in trouble and the imported chocolate didn't help. Must have been one of my worst days yet! Nothing worked. Everyone on staff either ignored or defied me so I gave them all a sermon about someone bad-mouthing me at a weekend party. My timing was perfect.

"That was me you were talking about! One of you made some vicious allegations about my so-called underhanded controlling behaviour at a Saturday night party. It was also mentioned that lots of staff would love to get rid of me – that fat cow MB! Well, it all got back to me and I'm warning you all to watch your professional conduct in public! I'm not condemning anyone in particular right now but you know who you are. Next time I will point out who the culprit is and make an example of this staff member!"

Yes, I was a crafty boss! I knew who it was but I wouldn't say a word. They were all behaving like kids – smirking, picking at some body part or squirming in their chairs. And I was sure the culprit sat in the corner of the staffroom. It had to be her. She was the only one at the meeting who constantly folded and unfolded her arms, as if she were pinned halfway between defiance and uncertainty.

Yea, those nuns taught me everything I knew.

* * *

At the Daycare Learning Company, I wore only designer jeans or cords and MB never said a word about my clothes being unacceptable or unprofessional or me being a toy doll. She better not say anything too personal because some staff around here wanted to chop off MB's head and use it for firewood.

Maybe she left me alone because I used to be a single father and had a five-year-old daughter but I didn't think the boss knew about my kid. My ex-girlfriend lived in Lethbridge, which was just far enough away from Calgary. She was also very possessive and wild-tempered. One time MB stood up to her at the front door because my ex insisted on seeing me while I was teaching – even though I thought MB might still be a bit cool towards me because she wasn't invited to my stag party awhile ago.

"Where's Michael? I demand to see him right now!" the ex. shouted.

"Michael is busy at the moment and can't be disturbed."

"Why not?"

"Because I said so. That's why," the boss said.

Ever since she secretly took karate lessons, MB challenged anyone and everyone to back off whenever she felt it was necessary. MB was also glad that I had finally got officially married to one woman.

I thought the relationship with my new lawyer wife was turning a bit sour too, but I hesitated to break off with her. Summer was coming and my daughter and I needed someone to go camping with us. Besides, my wife was not a violent woman, like my ex-girlfriend and I didn't care what anyone thought of my motives. I knew my values needed fixing but they could wait until the end of the summer. Loneliness was just too expensive.

It was time for me to go pick up my daughter at the other daycare that was not this school. Then, we'd head home to my wife's acceptable arms.

"Did you have a good day, Michael?" MB asked as I prepared to leave.

"Satisfactory," I said.

"Only that?"

"I have lots on my mind."

"Like what, Michael?"

"It's personal."

"Okay, as long as it's not affecting your job."

"Well, maybe I should tell you then."

"Tell me what?"

"I have a young daughter from a previous relationship," I said.

"Michael, I didn't know you had a kid! And didn't you just get married not long ago?"

"That's true. I bet you remember the argument we had in the staffroom about my stag party."

"I had forgotten about that."

"Anyhow, my daughter is a challenge. She wants her mom in Lethbridge. She wants me. And she's waiting for me to pick her up from the daycare."

"I guess you better go then. Have a good evening, Michael."

"I will," I said. "I will."

"Did I ever tell you that I really like those pants you wear? Designers, right?"

* * *

I had a quick step around people at the Daycare Learning Company but my eyes were tired today because I was worried. My past wouldn't leave me alone and I still got bothered too much about most things. My new beard covered my face like a bush and, except for my designer slacks, I wore clothes that came from a high end, second-hand consignment store. Nobody knew. Also, I had been known to eat anything that was placed in front of me and I heard a ten-dollar bill hit the sidewalk. Co-workers told me that I certainly looked tall, lean and must be in great shape. If only they knew. If only they knew that one of the reasons I was slim was because I made sure I didn't eat too much – a result of my days not long ago as a Greyhound bus driver when money was scarce.

At lunch today, MB sat next to me and began nibbling on her tuna sandwich while taking sips from her can of Diet Coke. Suddenly, she stopped eating when I said, "Want to try a bite of my leftover moose meat on white sandwich?"

"No thanks, Michael!"

Then the boss scooped up her lunch and moved to the end of the table with a look that said I should go home tonight, get on my knees and ask what's next.

Frugality. MB understood frugality or the reasons for my quick step. Her life was not concerned with gratitude for the moment. I lifted a slab of moose meat from the bread and flashed it at her, like a new found leather glove.

"Did you lose a glove?" I asked her.

"Keep doing that and you'll lose a job, Michael," she said. "Know why you're not too bright, Michael?"

"Am I hearing what I think I'm hearing?"

"You sure are!"

"Sounds like you're back to your regular self. Thank you so much."

"Don't you want to hear why, Michael?"

"Why?" I ask. "Why am I not too bright?"

"What's the similarity between a bird and a tree?" she asked.

"A bird lives in a tree."

"You're wrong. See, I told you, Michael."

"Then what's the answer?"

"They're both alive, Michael. That's called abstract reasoning."

"I don't know what to say. Your gifted intellect is so, so... overwhelming!"

"That's what makes you and I so different, Michael."

"The overwhelming or the intellect?"

"Take your pick."

"Wanna help me choose?" I asked with a small grin on my face.

* * *

"Hey, Michael, I love your tie but I'm curious, what are you hiding behind that beard of yours?" Louise asked.

"Not hiding much, Louise and thanks for your kind words about my tie."

When I looked at my reflection, I was reminded that my black hair was raked forward, like a fragile layer of topsoil and I didn't like the way I looked. My new wife told me yesterday, "Michael, don't worry so much about how you look because you're as gentle as the pink's and baby blue's in those twenty-year-old neckties you bought at the second-hand store. And you make the best Caesar salad in the world!"

She was a beauty that woman of mine! And not too long ago I thought our short-lived marriage might be on the rocks. It changed for the better from one day to the next when one night I asked her to learn one new thing about me and I'd do the same with her. That opened up our communication like never before. Go figure!

Last night I went out and purchased a brand new, fashionable, paisley necktie. Swirling colours of purple, green, red, orange and yellow filled the tie. Maybe, the new necktie would lift some of the depression behind my new beard. I saw what was happening recently around here and that was dragging me down the toilet. MB was desperate lately because more and more staff ignored her. My skin was just too thin for this job and being another one of Eric's introverts made it worse. I was losing more and more drive being around these people, especially with the way they treated MB – even though I would never ever let her wear something personal of mine, like a necktie.

For two days, the new tie made a difference. I walked around feeling lighter, more sociable and wearing a smile as wide as a legal file folder.

On the morning of the third day, the necktie became a heavy, rainbow-coloured sword on my chest. By noon, I loosened the tie, removed it and flung it onto a staffroom table. And the necktie stayed there, curled up in a delicate heap of colours.

Two hours later, the tie was still on the table and it looked better than my insides. When I left for home, I promised myself I'd go for some counselling; I shouldn't always be looking to ties as medication to make the gloom go away. The hopelessness couldn't be all mine and I should find out where it came from.

When I returned to work the next day, my rainbow necktie was still exactly as I left it on the staffroom table and remained there for several more days afterwards until MB suddenly scooped it up and flung it into a Lost and Found Box. Well, that did it! I immediately phoned and made my first appointment for counselling. When I hung up the phone, I thought of shaving off my beard too.

* * *

I had to keep busy.

And recently Angie said, “You know something, Michael? You are the very best at looking occupied.”

This afternoon I had a file folder, a ledger and a paperback book open on my desk. When I got up from my desk, I carried the file folder under my right arm, a black pen behind my left ear and the paperback book clenched in my left hand. I worked my way to MB’s office and made myself noticed. I nodded at Louise and other staff as I entered the main office area. And I saw that the boss wasn’t busy so I cleared my throat and she motioned me into her office, like any pleasant boss would do.

“Come on in, Michael. How can I help you?” she asked.

Her office was far too warm. I could feel the sweat already. Strands of my combed forward hair began to curl and I willed them to lie down to cover my high forehead. The strands originated from just above my left ear and when combed flat, gave my head the look of a dark floor-mat. I suddenly felt very self-conscious about everything, including the colour of my eyes and that cucumber nose on my face. The other day, Louise said my moustache, wildly flecked with shades of black, sprouted from my upper lip, like an exotic plant and could belong to a South American army colonel who assassinated would-be criminals for target practice. I also thought I had the slight beginnings of a pot-belly – even though I jogged, which wasn’t often enough lately. All I needed now was a sombrero and a cigar.

Today was Friday and I was wearing designer jeans. Occasionally, I stammered whenever I got excited and this was going to be one of those moments – even though I hadn't said much to the boss yet.

"Now what can I do for you today, Michael?" MB asked.

"I need mmm… more money to buy books. More than w…what my b…b…budget allows."

Within the last several days, my speaking had developed a life of its own whenever I had to interact with the boss, as if MB were pulling my strings.

"You're such a hard-working guy around here, Michael. Sure. I'll take the money from another budget for you," she said.

"Th…Thanks."

Leaving her office, I felt more determined and confident than ever. My hair was limp and the curl had gone. I was glad MB reminded me of my invaluable presence around here. I called my girlfriend-wife, at noon and told her what happened. And I kept a file folder under my arm when I used the office phone. In case. Just in case.

Upon returning to my desk, I heard a scratching sound in my bottom drawer. When I opened the drawer, I saw a gray field mouse dive under a file folder. As the file folder rustled this way and that, my hand froze on the drawer handle.

* * *

I could have eaten my niece up because I loved her that much.

She knew about me being a boss woman and that sometimes embarrassed me for several reasons – mostly because of how my buttons got pushed too often at work recently.

The other day I screamed at a boss man from another Daycare Learning Company because I felt his school wasn't doing a good enough job with my niece's education. I also blamed my niece for not trying hard enough; I thought she was a gifted child. Yet, my niece felt she was an ordinary kid and liked being that way. And her father, who was my brother, was becoming more leery of me lately because he heard through the grapevine about some of my escapades at the Daycare Learning Company.

Yesterday, I came over to my niece's home with a real school desk that I "borrowed" from my own school. All for a good cause, of course.

In earlier talks with my brother and sister-in-law, I convinced them that they needed to keep a solid reminder of school at home so my niece could work to her potential. My brother looked at me as if I were nuts and ignored me at first. However, soon my sister-in-law and I were drilling holes and we bolted the desk to the floor in a corner of their living room so it couldn't be moved. I was sure my brother thought I was from another planet but he went along with it anyway. And I made it very clear – when doing her homework, my niece was to sit at that desk. No TV. No music. No computer. No cell phone. Nothing but school work! Even her parents sat and read in the living room while the daughter did school work. No disturbances whatsoever. And nobody challenged my directions.

Well, my brother began reading more and more biographies and my sister-in-law doubled her number of Agatha Christie novels. Within a few weeks, my niece's marks improved dramatically. She realized that being ordinary wasn't good enough. However, she was never comfortable in her living room whenever I came to visit. I tried calling it a family, caring visit, a visit from my heart. Every time I came over though, I first wanted to know about my niece's marks, her work habits and what everyone else was reading, as if my brother and his family were my only mission. And whenever I came for a visit, there seemed to be something about the size of my heart that kept my niece frozen, between love and fear, as if she were captured on the cover of a horror comic book. But what the hell, a small dose of fear was good for anyone.

I could have eaten my niece up!

* * *

Nobody knows that I've had a few difficulties because of my past booze problems. My wife walked out on me with the kids and went to live with the keyboard player in a rock and roll band. Yet, I've been clean and sober for the last six years and I've learned to live without that controlling ex of mine. And I could now live with any new pain.

I was very sad today because my best friend, who also happened to be my ex father-in-law, died suddenly nearly two days ago. MB was really trying hard to get along with staff and she said, "Eric. I really admire how you speak so eloquently about your best friend's suffering and then his death. Was his death a painful one?"

"No, he went quickly in his sleep."

"It must be hard on the family."

"What death isn't?"

"Are you going to his funeral, Eric?"

"Of course. As a matter of fact, I was about to ask you if I could take the afternoon off to attend the service. It was planned at the last minute as most of these things are."

"Of course," she said. "Go ahead."

"Thanks," I said.

"Don't be shy to talk about it, Eric. I was reading somewhere that in the last fifty years we have learned to not be afraid to talk about... most of our secrets except for one – death."

"I'll remember that."

On my way to the church I assumed it would be no problem for me to pay my last respects. I called my ex-wife in advance just to be sure. However, her new husband was at the church door with the rest of his band members and did not allow me inside.

"I'm speaking for everyone, Eric," he said. "You're not welcome here – unless you want to argue with five guys."

I knew this was a lie. But I left as I didn't want to cause any kind of a scene. If this had happened six years ago, I'd have introduced the keyboard player's testicles to his nostrils. Instead, I thanked the new husband for his concern and trudged steadily down the church steps to my pickup truck across the street. Then, I climbed inside my vehicle, placed my head in my open hands on the steering wheel and very calmly, but repeatedly, whispered goodbye to my best friend. After I grew tired of my own voice, I turned the key in the ignition, wiped the burning from my eyes and sat up straight. As I slowly drove away from the church, the walls of each passing building looked as if they had a rare skin disease which was suddenly cured by my vivid sobriety at the next corner.

Next morning at the staff meeting, MB made a great show of acknowledging my distress and I wondered if it was her way of somehow making me pay for taking the afternoon off. But then she surprised us all by canceling the rest of the meeting and saying, "Everyone… needs some time alone."

III

FIVE O'CLOCK TRACKS

"We're buddies, Michael," MB said in a bar. "All of us here tonight are friends and I'm buying."

"Whatever you say," I replied. "How about another one?"

"Sure, Michael!"

Yet, her eyes spoke a different language than her mouth.

Under the soft blue light, MB bought us rounds of beer and smiled hugely. Was this the first time anyone sat with her in a bar? For some reason or other I had to look at her closely in the bar-room light, as if I were studying the bottom of my glass. I saw a woman of about five-foot-seven and at least twenty pounds overweight. She reminded me of an ever-changing cartoon shrinking and swelling in the neon light. As if she were reading my mind, she told us she nearly went crazy trying to lose the extra weight but now she didn't care. MB's eyes were a cloudy coloured brown with red tree branch lines spinning out from the centre. She was becoming more and more tired with each sip of beer. And soon her eyes were two large clumps of dead bush leaning into a pond. Whatever eye colour was left must be coming from the rays of a faltering sun. Yes, the fluorescent lighting made her eyes more watery now and the soft rock music together with the greasy smells of fast food added more fuzziness to her features.

"Remember, this is my treat," she reminded us.

"Thanks," we all said at almost the same time.

We each took a long swig from our glasses, as if we were drinking from the fountain of knowledge. Meanwhile, MB resorted to sipping and perhaps she could only gargle at the same fountain.

"Now, how can I make your jobs easier at the Daycare Learning Company?" she asked. We said nothing, looked at each other and then at her, as if asking why her eyes left their true colour at work.

"Come on, Michael, you first! What can I do to make your job run smoother?"

"Can we talk about it at work tomorrow?"

"You know me, Michael. I might forget by tomorrow."

"Why don't we just relax tonight and talk about non-work issues instead?"

"Know something? You're absolutely right. One last round on me!"

"You're making it all easier already," I said.

"You kill me, Michael. You young bucks are too much!"

* * *

Being at this event was so, so relaxing.

Animated conversations, the sudden pockets of laughter, the music and the snap and pssst of beer cans opening – all of these brought a lull to my brain noises. I lowered myself into a lawn chair right here and watched the tall, young, new staff member of Polish descent who sat cross-legged on the grass and forgot about being MB. Yes, she was the one who I've hired from another school for next year. What's her name again? Oh, yes, Lucy. Right, that was it. Her parents called her Lucy after the main character in the "I Love Lucy Show".

In one hand she clenched a beer bottle. In the other, Lucy aimed one beer bottle cap at another cap resting on an empty bottle in the middle of the lawn. The object was to knock the second cap off the bottle. She was determined to win at all costs and I questioned her motives from a distance. Was Lucy a loner? Did she have a lover who understood this beer cap game? Lucy said little and showed no emotion whenever she happened to dislodge a cap. I should have stopped speculating about Lucy because I didn't really know her yet and I didn't know a single Polish joke to help me understand better. And didn't I just tell the staff a few days ago that it was dangerous to live in a world of vanilla or chocolate?

One week later at a staff meeting, the tall, young woman announced to everyone that she would be marrying a Japanese co-worker from another Daycare Learning Company to make it a Japanese-Polish combination. In fact, he proposed to Lucy by taping the boxed ring to a basketball hoop at a game in his gymnasium and asked her to climb a ladder and help remove something that was stuck to the hoop.

Lucy invited everyone over to her place to celebrate the engagement with a beer cap-flinging contest on Friday. The young woman was so happy, she said, "Think I'm crying all the Polish tears I've been saving up since my Montreal childhood. And what a wedding it will be with Japanese and Polish in-laws unable to speak English to each other! Can you imagine?"

Her husband-to-be, who laughed at most small issues, accepted from Lucy and even wore, a T-shirt gift which read, "Have you slapped a Jap on the back today?"

Lucy did this to celebrate his gentle spirited humor and nothing more.

Privately though, he raged about the mistreatment of his Canadian ancestors and loved Joy Kogawa's Obasan and Itsuka.

"We don't all look the same but I pretend to let the jokes roll off my back by occasionally bringing the staff a free sac of Taber corn from my parents' farm in Taber," he reminded me when I asked him how he felt about the Japanese jokes. "I better let Lucy know too."

Her joy I loved! I could almost see where Lucy's humor originated beneath her tight, athletic-looking skin. Besides, we needed some new blood on staff next year. And I was so glad I took a moment to understand the infinite variables of beer caps and determination. At least it helped me to momentarily forget how staff members felt about me.

That night, my prayers included a Lucy skin transplant for myself and a desire that the staff never know about my petition.

And being at this event was so, so relaxing.

* * *

It was that funny guy Michael again. With that flashing smirk of his, he strutted into the staffroom ready to splash everyone in the face with another story. "Hey, did you hear the one about the guy with the one-legged wife who often said to her, 'Hop to it, Peg?'"

Then Angie replied, "Only you would… get that one, Michael. Incidentally, that joke is so old, it should be burnt! Why do you stick… with it, Michael?"

They said Michael's strutting was more noticeable when I wasn't here. If my being at the Daycare Learning Company cut back on his swaggering, then so be it and I didn't mind being called Missionary Boss.

Today, Michael was dressed in a blue tweed sports jacket, blue shirt, gray-knitted tie and perfectly pressed blue jeans. He really looked like one of those WAL-MART toy dolls.

"Know why I don't have a moustache?" he asked Angie and Louise.

"Why, Michael?" Angie asked.

"Because it made me look like a pimp."

"And what do you think you look like without a moustache?" Louise laughed.

"Thanks a lot," Michael said.

"Wonder what he's really like under the sheets?" Angie asked aloud after our resident comedian left the staffroom.

"Bet his young underwear is pressed too," Louise said tucking one hand into the other. "Probably folds his shorts in half before having sex."

"And his new wife works as a lawyer, so maybe she has no time to do the ironing or perhaps he does his own. Maybe his only friends are the Palm Sisters. Hard to figure him out because he goes on his horrible joke binges sometimes," Angie added.

But I knew Michael. He was deadly serious about his ambition to become a boss man in another Daycare Learning Company. Someone told me Michael had a brilliant mind and that he used humor so people would like him. It was that hide-and-go-seek maturity of his that worried me most. Last week, I told Michael that there was a sale on maturity syrup at London Drugs and his mouth full of teeth nearly dropped to the carpet. I couldn't resist. And he had it coming! Did what I said take the crease out of Michael's underwear and jeans? Was it enough to hear his new wife's wooden leg on the court room floor?

When I looked outside, two robins told each other jokes on a tree branch and I named the more demonstrative bird, Michael.

* * *

Because I had little success with diets, I kept changing my hair colour to see if that helped but it didn't. What a battle! I wanted to be slim and have long, blond streaked hair that never required touching up. In addition, I've also worked at being warm and forthright with others. More than ever before, I appreciated good clothes so I tried to be well dressed every day. Nearly everyone else around here said "Good Morning, Louise" but I was at the point where I liked to just say "Hi" instead because it felt as true as a handful of sunlight. I now had my own truth because of my new found meditation exercises. I slept well most nights. Not too many things at the Daycare Learning Company bothered me anymore.

Just as she was entering her office, the boss said, "Louise, you know recently you have demonstrated some solid work habits around here and have I ever told you that your presence in the Daycare Learning Company is greatly appreciated?"

"No, you haven't," I said, my voice somewhat stiff. "But thank you anyway."

"You're welcome!"

But somehow, I always felt she had a private agenda for me, like maybe MB waited for me to make one big mistake so she could pounce on me. Other days she wanted me to be a future administrator in charge of secretaries or something. The boss was always trying to convince people to go into administration, as if Central Office was paying her a fee for each new recruit. Hard to tell which side of her mouth she was speaking out of sometimes. Ironically, I knew she was struggling with many people around here; however, MB made her own bed so it was all hers for the sleeping.

For some reason, this made me think of my young daughter. Last night, she accidentally dropped my husband's solid gold wristwatch down the toilet. My husband wasn't the least bit angry. Our little girl could have dropped our entire savings down the toilet and he wouldn't have said a thing. And my husband loved the way I taught our daughter to say "Hi" instead of "Good Morning". Most times I still made her bed for her though. Wonder when I'll show her? Wouldn't want my daughter to grow up to be like the boss and have so many people at work despising her – all this because she never learned to make her own bed or sleep in the one made for her.

Several days ago, someone stole my purse including all my credit cards and cash. I wasn't too upset and immediately called Master Card, American Express, The Bay and Shell. My husband was angry at how MB suddenly blamed me for leaving my purse unguarded when, in actual fact I had it carefully stuffed in my bottom drawer under some empty file folders. The anger that followed her silence had a fungus quality to it, as if the rage were breeding a malignancy of sorts. Behind MB's eyes was a woman who wanted to peel away my skin and photograph my insides. And after she praised me for my work this morning, I wished someone... anyone could convince me that I was wrong about her.

And on my desk, the cover of the latest Cosmopolitan Magazine promised me results with a calculated diet of sin food.

* * *

I thought I was getting better but who knew for sure.

It was Friday afternoon and I walked into the staffroom dressed in my brown cowboy hat, skin-tight, yellow polo shirt, blue jeans and my flesh-coloured cowboy boots. This used to be my costume for the weekly raising of hell in the bar after work. I no longer drank but I still dressed this way every Friday to celebrate the end of the week. And most other employees at the Daycare Learning Company wore jeans on Friday too.

Most nights now, I lifted weights and gulped down a handful of daily vitamins. And I'm still jogging too. Presently divorced from my first waitress wife, I had visiting rights to our four-year-old daughter, Gina, who lived with her mother in Lethbridge. That little Gina means more to me than any Friday. Anyhow, I was getting married this time to my current girlfriend and hoped that being married for real would give me more time with Gina.

A few months ago, I joined a self-help group where I learned how to get my teenage brain caught up to my adult body and how to think of others first. Last week an incredibly wise woman in the group said, "Michael, adolescence can last from the age of twelve until who knows when and often beyond that, so allow some time to get well."

I turned and looked in all directions to make sure MB was not here in this Friday afternoon moment and she was nowhere to be seen. The last thing I wanted to hear about right now was the boss doling out another prescription of her "grow-up" medication. Then, I turned to Mick and told him about last weekend.

"I know, Mick. I know I just got married again a short time ago but… I met this really intelligent, gorgeous woman at one of those self-help meetings a couple of days ago. God, she was smart! Her brain could swallow mine with a single bite. She had a great theory about growing up, which did not involve ripening, like fruit. We got along really well and went out for coffee together after the meeting. One thing led to another and we ended up in bed together at her place of course. I made sure my fingers were light and slow because that was how I learned to please a woman. Like a stove, a woman required time to really warm up. And the thrusting – seven quick ones and three slow ones, seven quick ones and three slow ones and so on. Women always exploded before I did and they loved my unselfishness! I call it thinking 'other' first. And you should have seen what that woman did to show her gratitude!"

"Michael, Michael… I think you have more than me as your audience," Mick whispered.

Louise and Angie, sitting at a table behind us, had obviously overheard what I said and they smiled so broadly, their mouths, if stitched together, could be the lengths of both my cowboy boots.

I thought I was getting better but who knew for sure.

* * *

There was a storm in my eyes as I pranced into the staffroom, jeaned in the very latest. I loved to show off my body in tight pants.

"Nice jeans," Irene said.

"Yea, and who spray-painted them on you?" Louise taunted.

Irene and Louise teased me about my jeans because they both liked me; I was quite generous with my time and money when those women required either. They could count on me. Most people however, avoided me because of the way my mouth worked by itself. But that…that was their problem.

"I'm starting to gain weight though because I spend weekends sucking the brown out of beer bottles," I said to Louise.

"Then, you know what you have to do, eh Angie," Louise replied. "Put the plug in the jug!"

Thing was, I wanted to be thin and to be liked too but I loved my beer. And wasn't life a huge liking contest anyway? And sometimes I couldn't stop apologizing for what I did and didn't do. After, I was almost submissive asking everyone in sight for advice so I could give my mouth a rest. I forgot how many times I said, "I'm sorry". Go figure!

The other day, MB actually mentioned to me, "Angie, I know you come from a heavy drinking home because of your dad."

"And your point is?" I asked.

"Well, Angie, my point is you sometimes have difficulty getting along with staff."

"I have trouble getting along with staff? Me? What about you?"

"Now, now, Angie, don't be so defensive. I'm only trying to help."

I guess that made me dysfunctional – another of those tired labels. MB knew my father and how he joined that self-help group to stop drinking. She knew too much about me!

"So you know lots about my dad?"

"We used to work together."

"That's nice," I said turning away from her.

"Don't you want to hear what I know?"

"In due time," I replied over my shoulder and focusing my eyes on a new male staff member over in the corner? Look at how he was staring! I wondered what he knew about me, about my dad? He sure was good looking. Was he horny? I knew what I would do with him between the sheets. And I didn't mean the bond paper sheets used in the photocopy machine. Hummm! Naw! He looked like the analyzing type. Bet he was just waiting for me to find something in myself that I despised the most. I didn't need to look hard. Maybe, he thought my life was like art – a lie which made others realize the truth. Maybe, he… . Why didn't I just ask him?

There was no need to do that. Look. He got up from his chair and came towards me. His smile made my toes curl. I liked him. I liked him. And the chemistry seemed mutual. Hope he liked my shape as much as I did and knew how to apply his data processing abilities on a mattress.

Yea, there was a storm in my eyes.

* * *

Perhaps, I had to stop being the boss around here and just walk away from the Daycare Learning Company altogether. And then again maybe I just needed a change.

This morning Michael dragged his feet into my office and I had no idea what got into him. His face was peeling and made him look like he recently escaped from a leper colony without his medication. Actually, he had just returned from a Hawaii vacation. I wished he stayed there. He was angry and still reeling from the sarcastic comments made by several women in the staffroom this morning – something about his face looking like a perfect holiday map of blisters. Earlier, Angie even called him "Map Face". He shouldn't have joked about women needing to be chained to the stove. This guy knew better as he was warned on two previous occasions to keep his shoe out of his mouth. Maybe, Michael should start drinking again and guzzle himself out of his own misery. Even the men on staff were avoiding him because they saw Michael as being bad luck. Guys did that with each other.

And now he refused to do any extras around the Daycare Learning Company because of those earlier comments.

"I'm not appreciated around here," he said with his palms thrusting towards the ceiling. "Michael. Michael. We don't get paid to be appreciated," I reminded him.

All Michael really needed was to snap out of puberty but I said nothing more, nodded my head and remained composed. Then, he left my office, his shoulders hunched over and his bottom lip scooping up lint from my carpet.

After Michael closed my office door, I realized I really

didn't want this job anymore. That was it! I snapped open a can of Diet Coke and tore the cardboard and then the aluminum foil off a Cherry Blossom chocolate bar – items I could rely on. The Cherry Blossom was gone in three bites and the Diet Coke, tingling down my throat, helped me think clearly. I saw it all for what it was. Must have been all the Aspartame and chocolate! Yet, the supply of stumbling Michael's was never-ending and my job was really that of an over-priced mother hen and nothing more. When I started, I had great intentions! Then, I thought of obtaining a job as a WAL-MART greeter and rehearsed a smiling "Hello, Welcome to WAL-MART" in my make up mirror.

"Attention, WAL-MART Shoppers, Attention! Diet Coke and Cherry Blossoms will be on sale until the day I die!" I shouted.

"You okay in there?" I heard Louise ask from the other side of my closed door.

* * *

Some of the women on staff flirted with me and the men teased me about it. Actually, my sexual preference might shock a lot of people. Several guys on staff probably knew because I found it hard to maintain eye contact with men – especially if they were good-looking and even though I did have a new wife. Guess that made me a switch-hitter.

Yesterday, Louise embarrassed me when she said, "Michael, you have an actor's bedroom eyes and the good looks of a top movie star. You must have woman kicking down your front door!"

Ha! Yes, I did get along well with women most times and I did take pride on how I looked but that was about it!

Then, Angie said, "And Michael, maybe MB should charge admission to mothers so they could come and see how good-looking you are on Open House Night."

"Thanks, Angie. Much appreciated!" I said. "You're a ticket too, you know."

I'd rather be telling funny stories from my Nova Scotia childhood, like the time I farted while out fishing and forced my two fishing partners to jump overboard. After moving to Calgary several years ago, I still thought of that wonderful outdoor bouquet and the two guys gasping and choking in the ocean. I wondered if their lungs ever forgave me.

For some reason or other, the boss told me this morning that I needed more commitment to my job because women were always talking to me about one inch away from my face in the hallways. That comment stung for sure! I reminded her that I occasionally shared professional concerns with women colleagues outside my classroom.

"How professional, Michael?" she asked.

"Very," I answered.

"What do you talk about?"

"Oh, just different instructional strategies."

"Right," she said.

"Give me a break, will ya!" I snarled.

"You call that professional behaviour, Michael?"

Oops, I had better watch my temper; I've hid it quite well at work – except for the odd time in front of my students. I mean I came from a family of nine kids and I was number five. People argued. And I liked socializing, so what's MB's problem anyway? She's been grumpy with me all morning.

Only a half-hour earlier, I asked her to use her telephone.

"What for, Michael?"

"It's a personal call. All the other phones are being used."

"Sorry, Michael but I'm expecting a sensitive phone call at any moment," she said.

Even though I accepted her response, my teeth grinded against each other, as if my real response came from my storyteller heart, a heart whose sexual preference was one of a gray mountain named after Rock Hudson, a mountain surrounded by smaller, green-covered peaks and a pretend wife – again.

One of these tomorrows, I will tell the truth.

* * *

Some days I wanted to phone Central Office and tell them to send over a new me, a new MB. This was one of those times when I felt overwhelmed by everyone's subtle and not so subtle agendas for me. But momentarily Irene saved my existence when she sauntered into my office and inquired about the staff social fund.

"What do you need to know, Irene?"

"Just want you to look at these figures. See if I'm on track," she said.

"No problem. Let me have a look."

However, what she really wanted was for me to approve of how she managed the money. "Irene, your numbers seem fine to me. You did quite well with this budget. But you know you didn't have to bring it to me. This is a staff social fund.

"I knew that. I just wanted another opinion as I'm one of the geezers on staff."

"What does getting older have to do with being smart, Irene?"

"Maybe not much," she said.

And then it happened. Her laughter, which began from her toes and gurgled its way up to her throat, made me think of a winter stream. The stream was mostly covered with ice and snow but when I reminded Irene about the great job she had done, the stream suddenly melted and the water poured free and clear. In a small, stark way, her laughter was what I needed for a new me today.

What's that? Now, Irene told me about the hard time she was having because of the annulment from her daughter's marriage with her medical doctor husband. Apparently, the son-in-law was game for anything that was sexually adventurous and the daughter couldn't keep up with him. Because of all that, Irene's daughter had herself tested for AIDS several times.

"Are you feeling better now, Irene?" I asked. "Is your daughter okay?"

"My daughter will live. I'm just waiting until my first name means happiness again," she said. "Always wanted to change my first name to Joy."

"That shouldn't be difficult for you right now."

"How do you know that?"

"It's your heart," I said. "The size of your heart is bigger than your son-in-law's sex life."

"Thank you," Irene exhaled, followed by enough unvarnished laughter to make me want to swap insides with her.

"Feel like a can of Diet Coke, Irene?"

"Naw, let's have one of those Cherry Blossoms of yours instead. Forget the Diet stuff!"

"Right, this is not a diet moment."

* * *

My caretaker was a vital person.

He was also an artist, a painter and I wished he and his creative talents felt that way. In fact, I had two of his paintings hanging in the main office area so everyone could enjoy his talents. However, at the moment, his wonderful, friendly, Asian face seemed to be extremely depressed about something.

"What's bothering you?" I asked.

"We want children. My wife and I have been trying to have a kid for years."

It seemed as if they attempted every medical and non-medical approach imaginable to get pregnant. Many fertility tests were performed and both he and his wife were normal in all areas. He was ashamed and wished his creativity could be applied to the making of babies too.

"We even tried adopting a handicapped child. You would think that it would be easy but no, we were told we were not suitable candidates. Tell me how do you become a CANDIDATE? What does that word mean? Do I need a license?"

"Maybe you first need to figure out how to get your names on some kind of qualifying list from Social Services."

"Lists? Why should we worry about being on a list? My sperm is fine. My wife is healthy. What are we supposed to do?"

"I don't know what you and your wife can do but I sure

like the way you work around here," I said with a shrug trying to change the subject.

My caretaker usually wore beige running shoes, dark blue jeans, a short-sleeved cherry-red golf shirt or a flannel shirt with the sleeves rolled up to his elbows. Most days I saw him pushing his broom with the quickness of a darting forest animal. And he repaired items around here a lot more efficiently that any of those Mister Experts on television. At the end of the day, my caretaker took down the Canadian flag and folded it, like a scared object. Then, he gently placed the flag on an empty shelf in the supply closet, far enough from the harsh sun and possible spills from office items.

"This Canadian flag is sacred to me," he said.

"Is it as sacred as your paintings?"

"Yes."

In one of his paintings, the one closest to my office door, a fisherman uncannily resembling my caretaker, scooped water in slow, slow motion from his leaking boat. His chestnut eyes pleaded, as if asking me to stay forever as the boss at the Daycare Learning Company; he had to be the only employee to think that way. The ocean sky was filled with whales and the sun almost penetrated the fisherman's head. His hair reached up in strands with lives of their own, here and there to sleepy clouds. With slumped shoulders, he seemed to be asking why I was so focused on the painting. And before I could reply, the water inside his craft became the colour of sperm.

My caretaker was a vital person.

* * *

I knew lots of people around here wanted to get rid of me and that was putting everyone on edge. But Louise was getting moodier and moodier by the day which was adding to the tension in the office. After all, she was the head secretary and the first person everyone saw upon entering the main office. I needed a secretary who had some control over her own moody impulses. Yet, I was really trying to understand people better, including Louise. What I meant was I knew she came from an alcoholic home and had probably never grown up emotionally. Come to think of it, there were a few staff members around here who came from a house of booze or maybe drank too much themselves. I'd love to give them each a copy of those twenty, straight forward questions that anyone could ask him or herself to see if he or she was an alcoholic. And Louise particularly, often brought her personal problems to work, like a few days ago when she again complained loudly to me, "Did you know that my father still calls me a slut?" "Didn't you tell me that once before, Louise?"

"Right, I did. But he's still doing it and my husband tells me to ignore him."

Now, what kind of father called his adult daughter a slut? And what kind of husband would allow a father to do it?"

Yesterday, Louise told me she was taking a correspondence course in creative writing. I remembered reading that some writers were not well-rounded people; they saw obstacles as threats and not as challenges to overcome. Yet, there were times when Louise could be extremely empathic for other staff members who may be hurting with their own personal problems; often she was the first one to drop everything and screw up her face with sympathy, as if she suddenly became a poster child for the Red Cross.

Then again, maybe it was all an act because yesterday she arrived at work late after an early morning dental appointment and I almost wanted to present her with an Academy Award for showing the most pain after getting her teeth cleaned.

Just an hour ago, she told me again she doesn't really need her job because her husband makes lots of money in his job. I had to wonder because she wore bargain basement clothes to work everyday and I was puzzled as to how she spent her un-needed salary.

And there she was sauntering into my office! What did she want now? And what's that in her hand? Right, I forgot! I'm supposed to evaluate her next week. First, she had to fill out the self-evaluation component on the forms. Her face was filled with a tight frustration. Hard to know if it was just another of her moods, or she was unsure of her value around here, or both.

"I've filled out my part," she said.

"Good, Louise. The rest is up to me then."

"Call it like you see it."

"Want to discuss what you wrote first?"

"Would that make a difference?"

"It will help me do a more comprehensive evaluation of your work, Louise."

"Think I'll pass on that. Just call it like you see it."

"Are you sure?"

"No, but do it anyway, please."

"Only trying to do what's best for you. If that's what you want, Louise then that's what I'll do."

* * *

I meant no harm. I really didn't.

I was a tall man and weighed over two-hundred pounds. My large eyeglass frames were made of dark plastic. In combination with my toothbrush-thick eyebrows and brown eyes, my new lawyer wife said the frames made me look like a tall, friendly owl. I liked that. Angie, who was not known around here for her tact, told me last week, "Michael, your hair reminds me of a mound of black snakes but you still look like a movie actor!" "I prefer to say that my hair has a life of its own, Angie, like my hugging. "But thanks for your insight anyway," I said.

Old Mick, who was short enough to blow his nose out of his fly, poked fun at me whenever he got a chance, like yesterday when he said I should take my giant teddy bear routine on the road.

"Mick, your road leads nowhere. And… when did you say you're retiring?" I asked.

I wished people would understand that whenever I embraced someone, I was rising above the Angie or Mick crap around me or else I'd choke.

I was also hoping that two out of three of my own future kids would be adopted from Asian countries and I would love hugging anyone and everyone, maybe because of those kids. Yet, MB thought too many staff members had a problem with my hugging. I didn't get it. I knew I didn't participate in staff social events that much but that didn't mean I didn't care about Daycare Learning Company people. And I didn't feel like a sleaze! What was the problem aside from the fact that I was attracted to both women and men?

"People are getting the wrong idea, Michael" the boss said the other day.

"What do you mean?" I asked angrily.

"Some staff members are uncomfortable. You're a newly married man and you're a big guy, Michael. Furthermore, hugging is simply not appropriate at the Daycare Learning Company! We're all professionals here."

Now I knew why I never thought of embracing MB and why people wanted her out of here.

After the boss's comments, I said, "Can I buy you a Diet Coke and then we can discuss this further?"

"No thanks, Michael," she said.

Something told me she was about to say that it was her integrity refusing the free can of Diet Coke. Suddenly, I felt another of her lessons coming on, meaning that she wanted me to develop more honesty and values when it came to hugging. The only thing MB was missing was an orange crate or maybe a morality tree of her own to hug. Then, it hit me. Tonight, there will be a full moon, not MB's most giving time of the month.

"I hate full moons," she said several months ago. "They make me feel empty!"

"Why is that?" I asked.

"It's personal, Michael."

When I stuck my head out a window, I heard breathing that wasn't mine.

* * *

It was shortly after lunch when I met Angie in the hallway. She seemed to have a lot on her mind as she looked like she was bursting out of her skin, so I braced myself. As she chattered away excitedly, her eyebrows moved up and down, looking like they'd spring off her forehead at any moment, as if she were pushing an invisible button to begin a performance of sorts. For a quick second, I wanted to bury my index finger straight into her ear to get those Groucho Marx eyebrows to settle down.

I had to listen to her. She was going on and on about her invalid mother being near death and how the mother absolutely needed a sheet of half-inch plywood between her mattress and box-spring so she could sleep and breathe at the same time. And now, she was ranting about her husband, who wouldn't know what a steady job was if his life depended on it!

"My mother and my husband – feels like I'm caring for two kids," Angie finally said.

Then, she asked me if I enjoyed the tiny bag of candy left on her desk this morning. Not being able to resist, I exaggerated how sweet the candy was with my very best acting voice and moved my eyebrows up and down in rapid succession.

"Oh, Angie, that candy was so good – so, so sweet!"

Part of Angie's job here was to teach drama and shrieking laughter exploded from her, as if she learned quite early in life how to laugh and breathe in a theatrical world. Yet, the paradox of this woman was that she left me candy but also insisted on telling everyone that, although she loved her beer, she ate only healthy food; Angie brushed her teeth after every single meal, including her granola snacks.

"You look like you're trying to analyze me," Angie suddenly said.

"Why do you say that?" I asked.

"Just the way you stand there, like a factory boss, sipping on her Diet Coke with that thick head of hair cocked to one side and nudging her eyeglasses up with her forefinger to distract me."

"Didn't even realize I was doing it. You've got me all figured out, eh Angie?"

"No, not really, In fact, I don't take psychoanalysis too seriously because psychology controls us with the fear that we are crazy."

"I see," I said. "I guess I better put my can opener away then."

"What can opener?"

"The one I'm using on your head."

"That's the one," Angie said. "But I tell you I am not crazy!"

"Never said you were," I assured her.

"Right," she said. "Right."

In the hallway, the Coke machine's humming became a steamroller and Angie walked straight towards it.

* * *

I applied my honesty every morning, like lipstick, my family said, and then I headed to the Daycare Learning Company ready to put in a hard day's work.

"You look like one of those honest soldiers ready to go on manoeuvres," my husband said. "Could be," I replied with a tight smile.

When I arrived this morning, I promised myself I wouldn't shout at MB no matter what. She already had all kinds of pressure on her by other staff members who wanted her out of here.

But not an hour into the day and I was ready to tear a strip off her because she kept telling me what to do over and over.

"Don't forget to hand in that personal information sheet today, Angie," MB said with the sternest of faces. "And I need to have that sheet by the end of the day."

"You know, I don't HAVE to work here because my husband has a highly paid job and…."

"That's right. Just like Louise. You've told me that before. In that case, Angie, don't let me keep you here. And don't let the door hit you in the butt on your way out," MB said.

That did it! I ranted. I raved. I yelled so loud that other teachers ran out of their classrooms to see where all the shouting was coming from.

"YOU'RE SO FULL OF CRAP YOUR EYES ARE BROWN," I shouted.

"I want to see you in my office at lunch time," MB said, her voice shaking.

Then, the boss walked away from me towards the main office.

Three staff members immediately gathered around me in the hallway. Michael said, "Angie, you are worth it because you are constantly providing convincing evidence why people, like MB, don't know it all."

Then, Eric said, "Congratulations Angie, you are giving yelling more and more credibility and perhaps even making it elegant!"

After, Irene moved closer to me and I could smell the stench of a hundred cigarettes on her breath. She stared at me, smiled and then moved to about an inch from my face. Then, she wrapped both of her arms around me and murmured into my hair: "Angie, your yelling at the boss has just made my day!"

"Just wanted to remind myself and everyone else around here what is known and unknown about MB," I said, pulling away from Irene's heavy breathing so my stomach could empty itself on the floor.

"Yuck! Poor Angie! This place really is making you sick," Irene said with a look that redefined 'poor you'.

"Just stay right where you are, Irene!" I said wiping part of this morning's breakfast from my chin.

I applied my honesty every morning, like make-up.

* * *

There was my Librarian again. I heard her from far away. Her coughs were frequent and deep, her breathing heavy and labored. Each of her sentences was punctuated with gasps. And every library book might have a page dedicated to the Librarian's lungs, thanking her for not breathing in their direction. Books choking on their own words would not be tolerated. Yes, she was very sensitive about her books. So were her lungs.

Yesterday, after I told her that smoking will shortly be prohibited at the Daycare Learning Company, I thought my Librarian would panic but she didn't.

"I'll have to sneak outside more often for a quick smoke

and be careful how I blend in with my books when I return. And don't tell the boss," she joked.

"Sure, I won't tell me," I said. "I might not like what I tell me."

"YES, you wouldn't want to hear what you had to say now would you?"

Strange how my Librarian only knew how to preface any of her responses or answer any question with YES, as if she were a wordless woman surrounded all day by stacks and stacks of YES sounding words.

She wore mostly two-tone, flannel shirts, like Al on that TV show, HOME IMPROVEMENT, and dark polyester pants. She even gestured like Al did when he pointed at the camera. Her long, curly hair was the colour of coffee. Plate glass thick glasses sat on her nose in the middle of a pimply complexion. A raspy, chronic sore throat was her only complaint.

Each morning she was the first to arrive at the Daycare Learning Company and she prepared the coffee with great care. I noticed that she usually paused for a moment or two to inhale the sweet coffee smell before heading up to the library. Maybe, the coffee aroma helped my Librarian keep her succinct YESES intact for the entire day.

"YES, I may have to double my caffeine intake when the smoking ban comes into effect. Perhaps… no and YES, I'll be able to grab a few puffs by an open window in the library behind those stacks of books that require re-binding," I overheard her saying to the caretaker one morning.

"Don't let MB catch you!" he said.

"YES, I'm not too worried. MB understands – if you catch her on a good day. Besides, I like hearing her mutter to herself

– especially between gulps of her Diet Coke, which makes her sound more dramatic!"

I thought my Librarian was as wise as the silence in her books. I also thought I could count on her for support to keep my job. But after overhearing her words about my muttering and Diet Coke, I'll wait for that right moment to ask her – maybe between a YES and a cough.

I never knew who my friends were.

* * *

On a good day, staff members called me the Ultimate Music Person at the Daycare Learning Company because I often had a song making its moves behind my lips. Occasionally, MB watched me moving my mouth and tapping my foot at the photocopy machine and asked, "Angie, what song are you singing now?"

Sometimes, I told her. Sometimes, I pretended not to hear her question.

This morning, someone suggested that I get a few of us together to put on a show at the staff party tomorrow night and naturally I agreed. Right away, I thought of three staff members who could sing backup for me. I approached each with my lead singer's voice and everyone agreed with my plan that we would sing I Want You Back by the Jackson Five. It was an oldie from around nineteen sixty nine but my lips loved it. Michael Jackson was a boy… then.

After work, we rehearsed over and over and at the end of it all, it felt like my three back-up singers were on the verge of a nervous breakdown because I wanted us to sound, not good but perfect – absolutely perfect. Would they or would they not be ready for our performance tomorrow?

At the party, I charged into the staffroom holding a can of beer in my right hand, as a microphone. I felt like a traffic light unsure of what colour to flash. Literally dressed in red, green and orange, I strutted around the room gesturing at each staff member as I pointed to my three colours. My three co-workers then opted out at the last second and sat in the audience. I sang I Want You Back to the three of them and I sang louder than usual. Everyone applauded before I was done.

"Sorry about that but my three backup singers suddenly developed sore throats."

Some people remembered the song. It must have been a favorite for a few of the older staff members. I needed another microphone. An ice cold, Labatt's Blue microphone. And the boss had the nerve to ask me, "Hey, Angie, were you trying to sing the life out of yourself?"

"What do you mean?"

"Well, you sang like your existence depended on that song."

"Did you read my lips, MB?"

"I sure did!"

"And?"

"And what were they saying to you?"

"It was as if I was no longer the boss here and you wanted me back."

Right away the stone silence lifted, the room exploded with laughter and someone said, "Let's have another one, Angie."

* * *

The door to MB's office was partially open and there was something I had to tell her but I hesitated.

"Can I help you, Eric?" she asked.

"This is not easy, especially with you and me but… ah, why not?"

"What's not easy, Eric? And if I'm the problem then why do you want to share something personal with me?"

"Let's be honest. You and I are not that close but… I really need to share this with someone."

"Go ahead, Eric, but first, let me close my door."

"It's not about you. It's my wife. I don't… I don't love her anymore. All day I've been telling myself what I don't feel about my spouse and I need to tell someone else before the talking to myself makes me crazy."

"Have a seat, Eric. Want something to drink?"

"Sure."

I knew it was coming last night after I did my daily exercise. The sweat I felt next to my skin didn't feel right. The sweat was ice cold, not warm, smelly and exhilarating. It was not a "feeling good sweat" but rather a "realization sweat".

"I have never loved my wife. I mean she's incredibly bright and has a great body but that's it. She rarely shows her feelings and often talks too much at the wrong times, as if she's never heard of reading body language. And whenever we have sex, I think only of other women. I don't even recall proposing to her. Because I was afraid to be alone, I simply fell into our marriage. Now that I'm not afraid to be by myself anymore, I feel horrible about the relationship. And you know what? I'm not afraid of dying anymore. Sorry for unloading all this personal stuff on you!"

"It's between you, me and these four walls, Eric."

"Thanks. You know, I think people just don't know about your redeeming qualities!"

"That's kind of you, Eric. Wait here while I get us a couple of cold cans of pop."

After she left, I asked myself if I shouldn't be looking for love in the file folders on my desk rather than at home. Wonder what all these names and confidential information had to offer me? My mother often told me that I was unable to accept her love, like all the times I pushed myself off her knee whenever she tried to show me any affection? My mother knew before I did but right now… right now, I had to stop that committee of assholes inside my head!

Now, I envisioned myself standing by the water cooler in the staffroom wondering if that "realization sweat" had been waiting beneath my skin: for this very moment, for the cooler's deafening gurgle, for MB's door to creak open, for more intimate conversation.

"Come on, Eric, take a swig of this," she said, offering me an ice cold can of Diet Coke while closing her door.

"I better get back to work," I said.

"Sit tight. I told Louise we are not to be disturbed. And if need be, we'll get someone to cover for you."

"This pop hits the spot!"

"My favorite," she said. "Now… where were we, Eric?"

* * *

I was in love with a beautiful co-worker whom I nicknamed Vision. I realized that she was the real reason I had that talk with MB yesterday.

"Eric, I love when you call me Vision," the beautiful co-worker said to me the other night in a motel room.

"Good, because that's precisely what you are!" I said. "An apparition!"

As a child, Vision had no friends, except for farm animals. And however well she achieved in school, it was never good enough for her parents. Vision was intelligent, gentle, sensitive and kind. She also had this awkward beauty about her which was demonstrated in her dipping walk because one leg was slightly shorter than the other. But she was far more than just "good enough" for me and brought out my best qualities. And we had so much in common: psychology, exercising, peace and quiet, thinking, laughing, pineapple-grapefruit juice and all levels of intimacy. When we laughed together, my toes cramped and our chemistry easily made ashes out of paper. Sometimes, in the staffroom, we gave each other an electric look that I'm sure was noticed by MB.

Vision was married and had three daughters. Her accountant husband, who was trying to overcome an alcohol problem, believed it was all her fault that they fell out of love with each other.

"I've paid out far more than I've received from you!" he told her the other night after they had had sex together.

"You know where you can shove that ledger of yours, eh!" she replied rolling over to face the wall.

However, even though she couldn't recall the last time she didn't bury her face in his chest during their seven minute, monotonous love-making, Vision felt her husband maybe deserved another chance.

I knew. I knew. I was also married with two sons. My wife

and I passed each other in the dark and that was it! Everything I said about my wife to MB yesterday was true. That I knew for sure!

In six years I myself hadn't had a drop of alcohol and Vision admired me for my courage while joking that she was hopelessly attracted to alcoholic men, whether they were recovering like me or still out there drinking their faces off.

"Eric, if we were together, we'd be all over each other," she told me that same night at the motel.

Vision was a raging vision in the truest sense. The April issue of US MAGAZINE forgot to include her face on its front cover along with Candice Bergen, Princess Caroline and Michelle Pfeiffer. And in the meantime, I was satisfied calling her by her nickname because I had never met such a classic woman whose mouth I wanted to eat.

Maybe, Vision would demand more substance in her own life when she began to feel her rage, when she realized who was looking back at her from any mirror.

Tomorrow, Vision planned to book off sick so she could visit a faraway zoo by herself and study the cages for more answers.

* * *

I often studied the pores on Vision's face far away from the Daycare Learning Company and MB. Here in the huge parking lot of a truck stop, I discovered that Vision had become a victim of her own sadness because she kept losing more and more of her romantic idealism, of which, she'd been told by her husband, she had too much.

Vision's husband worked short hours and made big dollars as an accountant. She also felt he was not too bright about life and had too much time on his hands. So last week, he found a part time job driving a horse-drawn carriage downtown. He told her he was doing it for the extra money and he spent everything he earned. The other day, Vision found a Rolex wristwatch curled up in the toe of his dress shoe and she wondered what else was hidden in the house.

Apparently, the husband was also very restless and loved to be around horses and goldfish, the only living beasts he trusted. Last night, he had Vision and their kids as passengers in his horse-drawn carriage as business was slow. Each time they trotted by a certain intersection, a middle-aged drunk ran up to the carriage and admonished Vision's husband for USING horses. Later, the same thing happened again on another street corner and her husband kicked the same drunk in the chest.

That night at home, Vision told her husband to take a shower because the smell of horses was too much for her and all she really wanted was to have some great sex with a clean-smelling man.

Now, in the front seat of her red Valiant, Vision laughed wildly about something she did this morning.

"You know, Eric, I'm always the one who has to take care of my husband's goldfish and this morning I was so fed up, I flushed them down the toilet. I named those little fishies slicing through the cold swirling water after my horse-loving husband and his two wonderful brothers. Can you believe that now my husband's huge intellect believes his goldfish will thrive in our city sewers and grow to the size of sharks. Brilliant mind, eh?"

"Gifted!" I said. "By the way, who will feed him?"

"My husband or the shark?"

"Take your pick."

"Certainly not me! Maybe he'll make another killing on one of his accounts, Eric," she said.

"But then he'll really have to account for things," I said.

"Yea, and eat his profits too."

After we shook the laughter from our bones, I felt somewhat detached from Vision's life and I kissed her with a gentle half-breath. Then, I inspected more closely the pores on her face and each one appeared to be clogged. Every one seemed resigned to a life of never being safe near the pores of a husband who wore his manhood, as if it belonged to someone else.

When I looked out the window, the moon had dulled on a carpet of stars and a single cloud became a question mark.

* * *

Well, well, well… look at that! Even MB was listening to my story and she told everyone she was listening too. "See, I'm listening to Angie's story. See!" MB said to anyone within earshot.

Good for her, I thought. She must be proud of herself.

This was my story:

Two boys punctured a spider's web in my back yard on Saturday morning and my niece screamed a cloud from the sky. Then, those boys taunted my little niece and ran off down the street. "Your web is worth nothing." they said at the same time. "Nothing!"

As soon as I heard what happened, I ran outside and followed the boys to their respective homes. They just happened to live next door to each other.

"My name is Angie and I live a few houses from here. Please remind your boys that nobody but nobody is allowed in my backyard if no adult is present!" I told both sets of parents. And they just nodded their heads in a kind of semi-shock.

Back at my house, I consoled my niece in the backyard. We watched the spider finally emerge and begin the weaving of a new web section. A sliver of bark still clung to the damaged web.

"Did I ever tell you the story of Charlotte's Web?"

"No, you haven't, Aunt Angie," she said.

Before I was even part-way through the story, the bark thread floated down to the ground and the spider rested for a moment in its web.

"I love stories resembling life but hate it when life resembles a story," I told my niece.

"What do you mean Auntie Angie," she asked. "What comes first – life or story?

"I think you need to have life before story. Somehow, a story is based on life usually."

"You mean something has to happen to someone in real life before you can have a story?"

"Close enough!" I said. "Maybe, stories are not about events but about the people the events happen to. Am I making sense?"

"Sort of," my niece said.

"I hope so," I replied.

Strange. Maybe, it was because I only took one spoon

of life at a time. Any more than a spoon and I confused my love and my hate – especially when someone messed with my niece.

Then, MB told me she loved listening to my story and that it seemed so real.

"Sounds like a story called 'Angie's Web'," she said with a warmth in her eyes.

* * *

Watching Irene get caught off guard by the sudden appearance of her husband in the staffroom made me wonder about the dynamics of long marriages. But, as the boss, I welcomed the husband anyway and told him to help himself to a coffee before he slid into a chair beside his wife.

"Cream and sugar are over there," I offered. "Help yourself."

"Just had the brakes checked on Irene's car, MB," he said. "Two days ago when Irene was at the garage, a mechanic vowed that her vehicle required new brakes. But I took her car to another garage for a second opinion and the brakes were fine. And after I went back to the first garage, the manager promised he would fire the guy who lied to Irene. I'll believe that when I see it, is what I told the manager!"

Now, in the staffroom, the husband flashed his victorious teeth at Irene because he had again made a decision for his brake-innocent wife. And he was so, so proud of himself in front of this packed staffroom.

Meanwhile, a hunched-over Irene squirmed in her seat and offered her husband a sip from her tiny bottle of Australian mineral water.

"Hang on, Honey. I'll get you a glass," Irene said.

She got up to find him a glass in the cupboard but took extra-long to do it, as if she had too many glasses to choose from.

Irene reminded me of that kid slipping into a phone booth to escape the unending rain. I saw her leaning against the inside glass and her mouth pretending to catch impossible raindrops from her husband's impossible sky.

"Irene, can I see you in my office afterwards?" I said.

"Sure," she said. "Soon as my husband leaves."

Later, in my office, Irene curled her body into that momentary shyness of hers.

"So, are you glad your husband took care of your brakes, Irene?"

"Did you ask me here to talk about my brakes? What do they have to do with the Daycare Learning Company?"

"They just might affect your professional performance around here."

"My vehicle's brakes have nothing to do with my job."

"Anything can have something to do with your job. Feel like a Diet Coke, Irene?"

"No thanks. Tell you what – you take care of your Diet Coke and I'll take care of my brakes."

"Are you sure about that?"

"Absolutely. I may appear shy sometimes but I know what belongs to me and what doesn't. Want your door closed?" I asked getting up to leave.

"Closed," she said snapping open her Diet Coke can.

* * *

In my recovery, I too was still sick.

I didn't like the look of Vision today. Something was wrong. Even MB was staring too long at us in the hallway. What? Vision was ending our eight-month affair.

"Eric, all this sneaking around – it's just too stressful. I'm a sick woman and I'm also worried about my heart murmur!"

"What heart murmur?" I asked.

"The one I didn't tell you about, Eric," she said. "I've had it since I was a kid."

Suddenly, her first obligation was to a heart murmur, her three daughters and then to try and salvage her marriage with a non-loving, moody husband. So now I became just another one of her work acquaintances at the Daycare Learning Company. Maybe, her brain had a murmur too.

I was so angry and hurt that I was ready to reach down her throat and squeeze more murmurs from her heart. And I just gave her my definition of love on a slip of paper a few days ago. The definition read, "Love is a passionate concern for someone else's well being."

Although I'm married too, I proposed to Vision in a parking lot behind a Relax Inn. We always met far away from the Daycare Learning Company because MB noticed anything and everything. Anyhow, I should have seen the warning signs when Vision glibly mentioned, "Yea, right Eric! It's easy for you to propose because both of us are already married to other people."

I should have known but it was truly the first time I had ever formally asked a woman to marry me because I felt that I had simply fallen into my first marriage.

"I'd like every intimate object I gave you returned. I don't want any leftover links!" I said to Vision.

I can't believe that she was stunned by my request and she bowed her head mumbling, "I'll still have the memories."

Why was she so offended? She was the one with the "Yea, right, Eric".

Next morning, she brought back the intimate objects in a 7-11 plastic bag which included: two books with personal inscriptions, a pair of lacy, crotchless, bottle green, panties and my definition of love still on that same slip of paper. I took the bag from her and later ripped both books and panties in half. Then I tore up my definition of love into tiny, tiny pieces and flung the confetti illusions, together with everything else, into a big, empty garbage bin in the hallway, causing the can to vibrate slightly, like a noisy, tin heart. And I never saw those panties on her because, in my recovery, I too was still sick.

* * *

Now that it's all over, I saw that Vision's real mission in life was to make insipid proclamations to people like balding men rather than doing what she was expected to do around the Daycare Learning Company. Even MB cringed more recently whenever Vision opened her mouth. I knew I was losing my hair, but what made Vision a baldness expert anyway? Maybe, most of the men on both sides of her family lost their hair at an early age so she thought she knew something about male baldness. Hard to know where Vision's actual dullness began or ended.

Or maybe it started with how she looked. Vision's long, curly, brown hair was streaked with gray just above her ears and ran down her neck to hide in her half-hunched shoulders. If someone placed a hand between her shoulder blades, they would find the bars of a bird cage because the bones of her back were clearly visible when she stooped over, even under her clothes, as if she were rehearsing the granny in her.

Last night, Vision and her husband, with his own high forehead, went to an Anne Murray concert.

"Know what, Eric?' she told me. "I noticed that Anne Murray's brother. who was one of her musicians. was also losing his hair and I made a mental note to tell you about it when I got to work."

"Good. You should have waited for Anne Murray's brother after the show so you could rub his forehead for good luck. You're going to need lots of it!" I said.

"Now Eric, don't be so insecure."

"Actually, I'm not."

"If you say you're not, then you are."

"Ah, where would I be without your farm girl psychology? Don't answer that, I already know."

The more Vision talked about receding hairlines, the more I imagined her losing her own hair.

"You know I attended a minor hockey game last night in an aging arena that required many repairs. The rink reminded me of that normal, unforgiving, vast, saggy womanhood mothers tend to have after giving birth to three daughters," I whispered to her in the hallway. "Does that make you feel insecure?"

Well, this caused Vision to stop, question her balding expertise, drop her victim head and pout as she usually did when she didn't get her way or I didn't say what she wanted to hear. Poor, poor Vision!

Too bad she couldn't control her comments about men losing their hair. Her favorite cliché was that all men are insecure. Vision's perception was about as original as her face was unique. And why was I still calling her "Vision"? One last look at her eyes and I saw a blue-green, hungry colour that said she was never satisfied because of that sagging bag of flesh between her legs. Perhaps Vision was just another one of those sex-starved, middle-aged, drooping bag of bones who took out her vengeance on her unused illusions. Among other things, at least my own wife was honest and I'd be a fool to lose her.

Oh, there's MB's voice on the intercom. She needs me at the office. And her voice… her voice was persistent, like the one telling me it's all over.

* * *

Maybe, he was just lonely.

I'm worried about that guy who used to be an accountant I interviewed for next year. For some reason or other his countenance seemed like it was hit by a train. At twenty-eight, his face was cracked, tired and untra-serious, as if this day were his last and he appeared to be shrinking right in front of me. During my interview with him, he bowed his head whenever I challenged any of his beliefs, as if he were anyone's prey. After one get-together with me, and a second at his request, he insisted on a third to make sure I wouldn't forget who he was.

"Won't be necessay!" I told him. "You'll get a call if you have the job."

"But, I really want this position!" he replied.

"We'll let you know," I told him.

His eyes were depression-brown in colour and the blonde hair drooping over his forehead, belonged to a four-year-old child. Some staff members started calling the applicant "Boy" behind his back and he hadn't even started working here yet. Even Eric and that woman staff member he had had an affair with looked at the former accountant with wide-open mouths.

"Why don't we send this guy out into the neighborhood streets to deliver newspapers?" Eric remarked quite loudly in the hallway.

After the first interview, he took it upon himself to roam the hallways and unloaded on the same two or three women about his failed relationships with women outside of work.

"Maybe, you can help me. I just don't get women. I don't know what they want. Can you please help me?" he pleaded.

All of this from a boy in a man's suit who was almost a perfect stranger at the Daycare Learning Company.

"This guy's a piece of work!" Angie said. "He doesn't know anyone but already he's bleeding all over everyone!"

"Hope you don't hire him for next year," Irene said. "Can you imagine having to work around that kid?"

"Don't worry, Irene, I know what I'm going to do with this guy," I said.

Without any warning the next day, he walked into school, began roaming the hallways again and offered his help to anyone who seemed to be going through a real or imaginary rough time. This guy was starving for intimacy.

"Excuse me," I told him. "Our interview is over. This way to the front door, please!"

A few days later he showed up again and told me about the past weekend when his parents suddenly appeared at his apartment door so he didn't make it to our staff party, which he wasn't invited to in the first place. And how did he know about the party? He must have seen the sign-up sign for potluck supper in the staffroom. I wondered, really wondered what his parents had done to contribute to his behaviour.

After he left my office, I watched him pull on his jacket and he looked like he was cradling a puppy dog in his hands. The animal was picture perfect cute and its partially hidden leash seemed to end in the right pocket of his jacket. Just as he headed towards the front door, the former accountant aimed the imaginary dog's adorable face at any Daycare Learning Company employee showing any sympathy.

* * *

As the boss around here, I expected everyone to be there and they were.

This afternoon a big boss in charge of programming was presenting a seminar to employees about administrators being the keeper of dreams. And this morning, I overheard two staff members saying that any administrator claiming to be a keeper of dreams, was living in an oxymoron world.

Looks like the big boss recently shaved off his small beard and his goose bump-filled chin still appeared to be in shock. He looked stunning in his cherry-red, v-neck sweater; the colour alone would make staff pay attention to what he had to say. And he had this way of looking at people with a distinctive blend of both curiosity and compassion. His intellect was greatly respected and he was renowned for starting a kind of Thomas Moore, voluntary discussion group on books that included all administrators and staff from other Daycare Learning Companies.

When he began his presentation, the skin below the big boss's bottom lip almost shriveled up on his tiny chin. The presentation started well and his intentions were good as he showed us all a video clip from the film Blazing Saddles. His purpose was to demonstrate how counter-productive it was to live in a world of absolutes by having characters around a campfire discover that the new sheriff for their small town was an African American.

"What did that scene tell you all about expectations?" he asked.

Staff members squirmed in their seats and hesitated to answer his question.

"Are you afraid to answer because of how you see yourselves around that same campfire or…?"

"First, I have a question for you," Michael said.

"Sure, go ahead."

"Do you yourself have any dreams, like that new sheriff might have?"

"After working so many years in Central Office, I'm not sure if I'm still capable of any personal dreams," he said, shocking us all with his honesty. "Last time I had a dream it was a nightmare. I was worried about my wife and her breast cancer. It's in remission now, thank goodness. But I'm here today to talk about school administrators being the keepers of the dreams of others. My own dreams are part of a minority group, like the new sheriff."

I liked his honesty and smiled at the big boss's incredibly crisp, gifted intellect. And he knew I was on a mission to make this Daycare Learning Company the very best it could be – even though there had been several staff complaints about me submitted to downtown administration.

Towards the end of his presentation, the big boss became a boy sweating profusely in an oversized red sweater, flinging snowball after snowball at a wall covered with obscenities. The snow stuck to the wall for a short time. Then, the profanities showed through and it was impossible to ignore the message.

"Can anyone now answer my original question about expectations?" he asked.

"But aren't expectations like resentments ready to happen?" Eric asked.

"And when did you stop dreaming, Eric?" the big boss asked.

In the hallway, the Caretaker's vacuum cleaner whined louder than usual.

* * *

The long weekend was here and I was taking my family away somewhere. It was time for me to get away from that past affair with Vision and MB with her intense thievery of my time.

"Eric, are you going away this long weekend?" she asked looking towards an office window.

"That's right," I said. "See you on Tuesday morning."

"Going anywhere special, Eric?"

"Just away. Bye," I said over my shoulder.

"Is it a big secret?" she asked, still peering out the window.

"Nope. See you Tuesday."

I drove home and we loaded up the car. Then, the family

headed off to a farm/campground called Lonnieland, about eighty kilometers north of Calgary.

Almost at the campground, I noticed a couple sitting around a fire and their minds appeared to be starving for discussion. I was right. Rushing towards our vehicle, they immediately had inquiries for each of us as we got out of the car and unloaded our gear.

"How are you all? Do you have questions? What's it like in Calgary these days?"

After we set up our tent, Mr. Lonnie invited us over to their campfire where he asked: "Okay now, what really fascinates you about the world?"

"Everything," I replied. "Especially human behaviour."

"Really? Well, sometimes it can get lonely here and guests provide us with different windows on the world," Mrs. Lonnie said.

"She's right," Mr. Lonnie said patting a dog near his feet. "We love those windows! By the way, what do you both think of dogs?"

"We love them. Had a Golden Retriever for nearly twelve years," my wife said.

Mrs. Lonnie appeared to be a tough, intelligent woman. Her poise could calm a thunderstorm and she could be a news anchor person on the six o'clock news. She wore faded blue jeans, a faded denim shirt and brand new work boots.

However, Mr. Lonnie was the curious, anxious one. I could see how his large brown eyes widened after a question was asked. Dressed in work boots, blue jeans, a faded green T-shirt and a green and black checkered lumberjack jacket, he seemed to be trapped between an introvert and extrovert world. A gray, baseball cap looked as if it were permanently glued to his head. When the flames got too hot and Mr. Lonnie removed his cap to wipe away the sweat, an expansive shiny, baldness was revealed. And when he noticed me glancing innocently at his head, Mr. Lonnie quickly pulled on his cap and answered his own question about dogs.

Then, our host laughed silently when I looked towards him and the new sweat dripping down his face, like raindrops off the fenders of his tractor parked nearby. His cap remained on his head. Perhaps, the dogs at his feet wondered how much longer his hat would stay on his head – especially when I said, "I love spending endless hours around huge campfires."

Something told me, that later on, Mr. Lonnie will take his tractor for a long, nowhere ride. Reminded me somewhat of MB when she told me she was off to a meeting at Central Office, when in fact she was gone for a long drive with the window down and her classical music turned up loud enough to startle everyone but her.

* * *

There was Louise again with her new blonde hair curled so tight, her eyes almost squirted their zealot blue colour all over the staffroom floor. But she took great pride in her work and the Daycare Learning Company staff appreciated her thoroughness, no matter what colour her hair was – as long as she kept her self-righteous blabbering to herself.

Oh! Oh! I spoke too soon. She was at it again. Listen to Louise ranting about the profanity in a drama production she'd never seen.

"Horrible! Just horrible," Louise sighed. "That kind of language should not be allowed in public!"

Then, Angie said, "I saw the play and there are only two mild swear words in it – 'damn' and 'shit'. Not that offensive! And if the production were filled with profanity, the play would be labeled as sloppy because don't you think that swearing is a lazy way to communicate? By the way, how can you talk about something you haven't yet seen, Louise?"

"Doesn't matter, Angie," Louise said. "My friend saw the play and she said the language was immoral!"

"That's your opinion," Angie said. "And opinions are like rectums. We all have one!"

"Well, I'm different and I'm right," Louise countered. "And what's with this rudeness about rectums? What's with all this clever justification for inappropriate conduct? What an excuse for living that is!"

"What's happened to you this morning, Louise?" Angie asked. "Did someone nail you to a cross?"

"Everyone here has forgotten about suitable words!" Louise said with an earnest angel face.

Suddenly, the staffroom air exploded with air bluer than Louise's eyes.

"Hey, Louise when's the last time you had good sex? Maybe, you need your oil changed."

"Louise, wanna eat my opinionated mouth?"

"Louise! Louise! Read my lips, will ya! They are not saying 'Flock Off!'"

I had better jump in! Good thing no parents or volunteers were in the staffroom today. Louise was at a loss. She was too busy covering her ears to continue proclaiming to the staff about the moral entanglements of language. Then, her face became glued to the ceiling just as I heard at least five variations of "Flock Off" from various staff members.

"That's enough!" I shouted.

"That...," Angie said in a barely audible voice, "is only the beginning."

* * *

"Know something, Jim? You're a small man consultant with a big heart and graying hair that looks like a stack of knitting needles and I love you," my wife said to me one morning over breakfast.

"You're a beauty," I reminded her.

"Soft knitting needles, Jim," she reminded me. "Very soft needles. And more recently, I've been concerned. Your skin feels like it belongs either to a frightened deer or a jittery rabbit."

"Fear not! And your husband, Jim, loves you," I said. "So do that scared deer and jumpy rabbit."

Having almost lost her total vision lately, I didn't mind what my wife said. I really didn't. Tolerance and love were what I was practicing with her.

"I'm off to the Daycare Learning Company. I'll see you later."

"Don't forget that lunch you made for yourself."

"Got it."

"Love your knitting needles and your new, long coat."

"Thanks!"

After my morning meeting, I drove to the Daycare Learning Company, back into my role as a travelling consultant to talk to MB. I wore my brand new long, fashionable winter coat, which occasionally made me feel like an overdressed clown. Being so short, it would take me a while to get used to the coat. I slipped it off and slid my brown-bagged lunch onto the table. Starving. Gotta eat! I unwrapped my uncut leftover roast beef sandwich and took a bite.

"Want a cup of coffee with that, Jim?" MB asked as she slid into the chair beside me.

"And how's your wife?"

"Getting there," I said.

My wife recently lost all her sight because of a freak accident when some laundry bleach splashed her in the face. It was horrible! Now, my fiercely independent partner had to be led by the hand to and from places until she learned to navigate alone with a white cane. We might get a seeing-eye dog too. I really tried to be tender when helping her get dressed but it just about killed her when I helped her slip on her bra. I knew she could do it herself but…

"Aw, let 'em hang out there by themselves, Jim," she muttered the other day.

Then, I used my kindly rabbit ways to place each of her arms in a blouse but her clenched fists sometimes made it difficult.

I wouldn't dare tell MB about all these details because the more open I became, the more deer-like I felt and the more uncomfortable she got. And I didn't belong in her headlights.

It was time for me to gulp down the rest of my leftovers. Then I rolled up my own sleeves and got down to my consultant work of reviewing a student's Cum file. Recently, I'd been feeling like I asked a cop to borrow his gun to rob a bank. Too timid. I was becoming a hybrid rabbit-deer from being too nice to everyone.

"Jim… Jim! Are you okay?" MB asked.

"Sure. Sure. Wanna run your fingers through my knitting needles?" I asked.

"What was in that sandwich of yours?"

"Leftovers."

Then I turned away from MB and listened to the lovely sounds of my chewing.

* * *

Terrified, I imagined myself now retired and coming back to visit the Daycare Learning Company to pick up Irene and take her out for a coffee and doughnuts at Tim Horton's. Irene and I were presently the oldest staff members and we had lots in common, like the times she told me when her brain nearly exploded in her classroom or with staff. All of this because of our mindless jobs as neurotic, defensive mother hens in an overpriced daycare centre and pretending to be someone we can't be.

"You know, Mick," Irene said. "I seriously don't know how many times I felt like telling the kids to just keep throwing spitballs at me and caught myself mumbling at the onslaught of paper."

"That's not so bad, Irene. A couple of weeks ago, this kid told me to "F" off under his breath so I grabbed him by his shirt collar and nearly pulled out some of his long hair as I pinned him to the wall. Something snapped inside me!"

As I was waiting for her, I walked into the staffroom and poured myself a coffee. I placed my cup on a table and headed to the washroom. For some reason, I couldn't smell anything today. Odd! Looking into the washroom mirror, I patted my stomach repeatedly and asked myself, "Hey Mick, how come you're not getting fat from retirement?"

With each sip of coffee seeping down my throat and skinny neck, my Adam's apple felt as if it were swallowing itself. I wanted to talk to someone, anyone, but the only person in the staffroom was MB. And as the boss around here, she was paid to sometimes listen, I suppose.

"I love my beer, especially with all the free time I will have," I told her.

Then, I again wondered aloud when my beer belly will show.

"I have no idea about beer bellies and retired men," she said. "Besides, Mick, you haven't retired just yet."

"Think I need to find another job soon such as hauling freight or the free time and beer might kill me."

"Mick, Mick! Hang on, you're not finished yet!"

"Yea, I know. I'm just trying to imagine what it will be like when I retire. I keep hearing that humming of fluorescent lights."

Maybe, I will love the sound of a truck's droning as it brings me ease on long stretches of road. Beer alone won't do that. And watching TV all day might make me crazy because the ceiling lights in my rumpus room are already grinding me up, like a dozen low-speed electric saws. And my wife tells me I have poor social skills. Maybe, it's because of that principal's job I had for a few years up north. Maybe, I…

"How can fluorescent ceiling lights do that to you, Mick?" MB asked.

"It's their noises. They don't belong to my night or day," I said.

"I don't understand, Mick. And maybe, you better get yourself another job when you retire."

"After this, I plan to," I said.

Suddenly, I smelled coffee in the air. Irene was ready. And everything was very clear.

* * *

I had less than a year to go before I retired from the Daycare Learning Company. Every Sunday I counted down the weeks before I drove to my church and sang in the choir. As a soprano, I sang away each day from the previous week of work and felt like a angel when I was done. Everyone in the choir knew that I couldn't wait to leave my job and they occasionally said, "Irene, we're singing loudly for your happy retirement too in the not-too-distant future!"

MB also attended my church. If I looked over and saw her seated below, I increased my own singing volume to its loudest. At least once, she looked up and smiled when she recognized my soprano voice above the others. I didn't sing for her, though you'd never hear me say that at the Daycare Learning Company. Like a guardian angel, I sang at her to protect myself. That's right. It was my way of wondering aloud when she was going to be transferred and take her control elsewhere. A few staff members mentioned yesterday that they were thinking of hiring a taxidermist to have the boss stuffed with candy.

"Then, we'll have MB mounted on that telephone pole

outside the front door, like a pinata" someone added. "And you know the rest."

"Ah, but she's not all that bad," Eric added as he walked by. "She has a good heart."

This Sunday morning, I had a horrible cold but still showed up for choir. Finding it very difficult to sing away the past week, I looked down at the congregation and simply hummed along with the other members. MB just happened to look up and pointed to her throat and then mine. Then I thought I saw her lips saying, "Irene, you are so hard on yourself? Go home and get some rest!"

After she made that pitiful face for me, the boss threw up her hands. Next, she folded her hands in prayer, leaned them tent-like against her right cheek and then pretended to fall asleep on them.

"Go home," her mouth repeated.

If I could retire now, I would but I used to be a nun for many years and left the order. Now, I'm forced to work until sixty-five to collect a full pension. MB knew this but still drew an imaginary slash line across her own throat with an index finger. I knew what she meant. Turning my head back towards the choir, their volume increased and I muffled my cough in a forced holiness of hand on mouth. Finally, I left and searched for a drink of water as the song inside me became a dying plant and the choir sang louder and louder.

"God bless you, Irene," a man in the back row of the choir said as I left.

"Thank you," I whispered. "I could use a favor or two!"

"Not sure if God does favors. Let's call it something else."

"How about if I tell God that I expect miracles?"

"That might work, Irene," he exclaimed with his right index finger pointing upward.

* * *

Yea, it's me, Mick the guy who was also about to retire. Thought I'd eat lunch with the rest of the staff today.

In a corner of the staffroom, Angie, who I'd grown to treat like a daughter, wanted to have a Cribbage game with me. We got going right away as there was only twenty minutes left in the lunch hour and it was just a matter of time before MB called me or Angie on the intercom to come to her office for one reason or another.

I nudged my eyeglasses closer to my face and thought of my wife who was dying of pancreatic cancer. She had three months to live. Not much time for suffering or the painful treatments. I was glad but not glad. My eyes reddened and watered up to their brims.

"What would you do if you were me, Angie?" I asked rubbing my eyes.

"Don't know, Mick. I… . Want to finish the game?" she asked.

"Good idea."

"Why don't you tell me one of your hilarious jokes?"

"Can't think of one right now."

The Cribbage board told me I was ahead by about fifteen points. I considered my early margin and decided to talk about my wife instead.

"You know something, Angie? I always bought her disposable gifts such as flowers or chocolates but all these years her childhood poverty really wanted me to buy her clothes. I only found out about this two weeks ago when the cancer was first discovered and my wife told me she preferred underwear to chocolates."

Then, I wiped my eyes and asked Angie why secrets waited so long to emerge and why I had this sinking feeling of a new kind of poverty in the pit of my stomach.

"There probably is a strange kind of poverty after death," Angie blurted out. "And more importantly, there's that pain right now."

"Fifteen two, fifteen four, fifteen six, fifteen eight and four is twelve. I can still count. For now anyway."

"You sure can, Mick. Good game. I'm getting skunked by a pro!"

"Aw, that's MB calling me."

"Let her wait, Mick! Same time tomorrow?"

"Only if you let me skunk you," I said.

"You won fair and square, Mick. I didn't LET you do anything!"

"Wanna hear that joke now, Angie?"

"Wait. Let me imagine the punch line first."

"My proctologist called an hour ago," I interrupted.

"And?"

"And he knew exactly what to say."

"Which was?"

"He found my head."

"Your joke cracks me up, Mick. And that's really cheeky of you in the face of death."

"And you, Angie remind me of a woman I knew thirty years ago."

Just before the bell rang for something, a boss voice called me again. And the ceiling language was calm but succinct.

* * *

As the secretary around here, I occasionally got the chance to see a different side of MB. And today, by accident, I discovered that she loved Golden Retriever dogs. When she talked about her two dogs, she simply became a big woman with a huge heart. MB even looked different in my mind. With a relaxed face, she smiled easily and her voice became melted butter. I saw her dark hair becoming shinier and her figure looking trimmer and much younger than that of a fifty-something-year-old woman.

"I didn't know you liked dogs so much."

"I'm crazy about dogs, Louise," MB said. "Always have been. I prefer them to people."

"Why Golden Retrievers?"

"Because only a Golden Retriever wags its tail instead of its tongue!"

When MB spoke of her two pet dogs over lunch today, she slowed down her speech to an easy summer breeze. She became more articulate, less machine-gun like; her eyes widened, and swept back and forth, like secret floodlights from somewhere inside her. Yet, when someone changed the subject and asked her a personal or professional question about anything not related to dogs, her face immediately changed with eyes staring straight at the person and measured words fell from her mouth.

"Did you just buy that gorgeous suit you're wearing?" someone asked.

"Yes, I have to look professional," was all she said.

That's it. No thank-you. No chitchat.

Now back to dogs.

After lunch, MB lightly got up from her seat in the staffroom, as if she were made of feathers.

"You know... Golden Retriever dogs always make me smile so profoundly," she sighed before walking away.

Then, she strolled back to her office with her left arm slightly ahead of the rest of her, as if she were doing figure eights with one of her dogs between desks, chairs, filing cabinets and computers. I watched her head turn to the left and look down at the carpet. Finally, her lips moved quickly just before her face became an enormous smile. Later, I wondered if MB would allow all employees the pleasure of having their pets sitting on the carpet right next to their elbows because the most beautiful change a Daycare Learning Company employee could experience would be the mystery of love on four paws.

* * *

Oh, there was Mick again.

He had such a short time left before retirement. In the staffroom this morning, he rested in the softest chair while the lazy alphabet of his cigarette smoke shaped the words he planned on leaving behind and the words he planned to take with him.

"What do you want to be remembered for, Mick?" I asked.

"Maybe how I made people feel," he replied without thinking. "Dogs make people feel."

"I know. I know. Why is that?"

"Dogs will not be remembered for what they accomplished or what they've accumulated but how they made people feel."

"I didn't know you love dogs as much as I do, Mick."

"Sure, I love dogs. I trust them too. We never talk about it. However, I also like to be left alone for a few minutes before starting my workday."

Meanwhile, as the boss, I couldn't wait until smoking was banned completely in a few months time. Everything should be done to make this place into a healthier working environment. I kept telling Mick about the future ban but he always responded by blowing extra smoke from his nose in my direction, as if he were some kind of Daycare Learning Company dragon.

"Better get ready to smoke outside soon, Mick!" I said.

"Yea, yea, Boss," he grunted.

His face was so wrinkled because of the constant squinting brought on by his cigarette smoke that I thought his cheeks and forehead would soon fold over themselves. His silver hair was a nest of baby, gray-black snakes combed like one of the Everly Brothers and his eyes were never fully opened. When he spoke, his voice was hoarse and broken by deep coughing fits. I didn't think he'd make it to retirement. And behind his smoke, Mick seemed like he needed to take a short nap every two hours. Now, if only his smoke could shape a bed for him right here, right now! I'd place him and his gray bed in the supply room and leave him there to snooze away the day in a darkened corner.

When he finally stood to start his day, Mick loomed up through the smoke, as if he were an aging beast pushing through a dense fog and the volume of staffroom chatter increased rather suddenly. While at the doorway, he paused and then acknowledged everyone with breathing that was heavier than gravity itself.

"Time to get to work," he said coughing and then spitting into his handkerchief.

* * *

My boss days may be numbered. I found myself in the hospital for testing and some serious rest. For so long, I've been worried that I wasn't wanted at the Daycare Learning Company. Half of my mind was probably here to forget the mindless dread of being pulled in so many directions at once and the other half wondered about the resentment I felt towards staff, myself and downtown administration. Not one staff member came to visit me in the hospital. Not my assistant, Eric.

"Surely, there have been some redeeming moments," my doctor said. "Can't be all that bad! And those colleagues of yours have to fill your shoes at work."

She was right. I've had some wonderful moments when staff trusted me enough to come into my office and confide in me. And I've had a few giggles when sipping on a cold can of Diet Coke alone in my office.

"Think of something that you're thankful for," my doctor added on her way out of my room. "You might need to feel some gratitude."

Yet, I'd first love to lose my panic thinking about returning to work. These thoughts have taken my brain hostage and I became ill, which was why I was here. Feeling grateful was like feeling subservient to someone. Just not me.

In the bed next to me, an eighty-year-old woman named Pamela was losing her memory. I'm glad Pamela was here, even though she was constantly twelve hours behind the actual time. Yesterday, Pamela's four-year-old great-grandson held her by the neck and told his grandma that her neck was sagging. He also said that her neck could be fixed with time and masking tape because memory pieces, like all body parts, could easily be taped back together again.

Pamela used to be a dentist in the Korean War. Says she used to fix a soldier's teeth by pumping an engine with her right foot to keep the drill going.

"Felt like a woman dancing in two different rooms at the same time – one a room of uncertain pain and the other a place where a relentless polka played on and on," she said. "Other times it felt like two different dance floors in the same room."

According to Pamela, she was in the hospital, not because of her job, like me, but on account of a constant mysterious aching in her left ankle. And there was also her memory which "had holes in it", like her white woolen socks. Later, I took Pamela down to the patient lounge to watch the hockey game.

In front of the television that night, I listened to Pamela's polite clichés about hockey such as "Wish they'd enforce ALL the rules" or "those men are overpaid!" All these words came from a woman who had no memory of how she became polite. When she got up from her chair at the end of the first period, she burped and farted incessantly and either didn't notice or didn't care. Maybe, that was Pamela's way of distancing herself from the noises of others. When she returned from her bathroom break, she asked me, "Want to come back to our room for a game of Gin Rummy? The Flames are going to win anyhow."

Back in the quiet of our room, Pamela's memory became incredibly sharp for remembering Gin Rummy rules and she was almost cocky about winning.

"How about teaching me some ways to cheat, Pamela?" I said chuckling.

Instead she said, "Yes, I've done quite a few dance floors in my time but if you keep moving, no one can hold on for very long."

* * *

In her paisley dress, the replacement for MB was a clock whose springs were about to erupt from its back. Those colourful designs and shapes zipped off in all sorts of directions and she seemed to be like that under her skin too.

"You better slow down before you vibrate out of your dress," I said after only her third day.

"I'll be fine, Louise. You just take care of the secretarial work!" the replacement said.

That was the first and last time I gave MB's replacement any helpful advice.

Her name was Noreen and she wouldn't last long. Noreen was short, had fading blue eyes, and wore eyeglasses that looked like they had been on her face since birth. Her dull curly hair was tied back in a bun, like her strained, urgent voice. Noreen's nose was beak-like and she was chinless. Yet, Noreen was as hard-working as they come and had a heart the size of one of those vending machines in the main hallway. I wish she weren't so intense because that already irritated so many of the staff after only three days. Today, I overheard staff calling her a neurotic weasel because of her long nose and chinless face. Noreen meant well but was addicted to perfection and would never settle for the notion of progress. Maybe, her quick mind wouldn't allow her real joy because society controlled her with the fear that she was worth less than others. It was hard to know for sure but she showed me so much about herself in such a short time and I was just the secretary.

Today, at lunch, Noreen opened her brown-bag lunch and ate most of the first half of her crust-trimmed sandwich. Suddenly, she was called to the main office and she literally ejected herself out of her chair and ran out of the staffroom. Right away, Angie tore a large corner off a memo lying on the table and slipped the paper between the bread slices of Noreen's unbitten half-sandwich, thinking nobody saw what she did. But most staff members caught it all and said nothing. Moments later, Noreen returned to her sandwich and the staffroom was suddenly quiet. She looked around and was unsure what to make of the silence. As soon as she bit into her ham and paper sandwich, staff members pretended to look the other way and exploded behind their hands. I noticed that Angie was about to confess to the prank but she decided not to at the last second.

"Hummm! This ham sandwich tastes like... like paper!" Noreen said trying to appear calm.

And she responded as if she were used to jokes being played on her. Noreen lifted her sandwich bread, removed the remaining paper and practiced her rehearsed smile, the kind you might see at a sales promotion, so she could think she had rapport with staff. "That's a good one," Noreen said. "I must be on the same page as everyone here."

"Oh, we all know what page you're on," Angie said.

There was now a strange, subdued glow on her paisley dress; maybe because Noreen's head and heart were huddling together to plan a response to the next prank. Or, perhaps a quick phone call to her ventriloquist, who was in the hospital recovering from this place, would tell her what to do next. And the clock's ticking became louder and louder.

* * *

This secretarial work never ended so I often took a break. Pretending to work by having a couple of file folders open on my desk, I was often observing how people behaved around here.

And there was MB just out of the hospital and back at work. At least, her replacement, Noreen was gone though. One more day with Noreen and we all would have had developed unheard-of nervous disorders.

The boss was way overdressed today, as if she were attending a formal event. Already, she was dropping her eyes, tightening her forehead and confessing to nobody in particular that her face was a real map of her feelings. Wow, this was something new for MB! But then, she lowered her voice to the level of a trombone and reminded Eric that nobody, but nobody should leave work before five o'clock. Eric turned to face MB and said, "That's a silly policy, a waste of time! If a job is done for the day, why can't someone head home a few minutes early?"

"You know something, Eric… you're right!" MB smiled.

"Do you have a second?" I interrupted. "I want to talk to you."

"Be right with you, Louise," she said. "Excuse us, Eric."

"I need to ask you something!"

"Sure Louise."

"What's happened to you?"

Then, just like that, without giving me an answer, MB turned away and approached Eric who was standing nearby. She stood just inches from his face looking like she was ready to fondle Eric and then take him home for the night. Maybe, she was reliving that staff party from awhile ago. Something had happened to the boss.

Today, MB seemed like a retired gunfighter posing as an elegant woman on a leash, and who was daily brought to an art gallery by her two, graceful Golden Retriever dogs. Her arms were bare. She wore a yellow, low-cut, chiffon dress and her over-jeweled hand rested on her hip. Silver high-heels clung to her feet, as if they were painted onto her skin. A diamond necklace hung like a lighthouse over her breasts. I saw her screwing up her face again, like she did with more and more frequency before she went into the hospital. Maybe, there was a person hiding with a camera behind the largest painting in the gallery who never worried about leaving before five o'clock. I hope the photographer captured her pose. Beneath MB's sagging face was a new, resigned determination that challenged the slightest wrinkle on her forehead.

Forget the art gallery! Maybe, she was really only a sidewalk pedestrian trudging through a big city snowstorm without any Golden Retrievers, here at the Daycare Learning Company.

The hood of a parka covered her head and she was the only walker with eyes perfectly level. MB didn't need to lower her face against any of the elements and her look was child-like in the blowing storm. Her eyeglasses were partially covered with snow and her arms were extended while a huge, black leather purse dangled from her left arm – an anchor in the wind. The woolen mitts covering MB's hands were as thick and pliable as they needed to be. Eric stood by her side with a new ease and together they laughed themselves silly in their five o'clock tracks.